Tilt Time

R. Vincent Tibbetts

Tilt Time

This book is a work of fiction. Any reference to events, real people, or real locales is used fictitiously. Other names, characters, places, and incidents are the product of the author's imagination, and any resemblance to actual events or persons, living or dead, is entirely coincidental.

DEDICATION

To whoever pulled off the heist at the Drake Hotel, New York City,
July 29ᵗʰ, 1973

ACKNOWLEDGMENT

In no particular order of appreciation; Stan 'the Man' Garber, John Gasca, Michael Uribe, Stephanie Zappalac, Naz Harounian, Todd Cernecky, David Susko, John Stevens, John and Christie Downey, Dan Pulskamp, Laura Streicher, and my brother, Timothy Tibbetts. Good looking out, one and all.

Those who put eyes on the project, Ariel N, Manta Menon, Jennifer Park, and Silvia Curry. Editing and cover art by the very talented team of Tanya and John Besmehn of Bezuki Services. I appreciate all your efforts in getting me through the process of breathing life into this work.

Special thanks to Jacques Auger.

I lost two friends in unrelated incidents while writing this manuscript and wish to acknowledge them here. I really cannot believe they are gone.

Jonas Lagunoff

Jesse Austin

If I could only go back in time.

Prologue

Historians have denoted the introduction of time travel to the general population as the Great Social Splintering. How such a schism could have evolved is up for debate. People within the present cling to their opinions and bolster their positions with contemporary facts. The job of the historian is much more sublime, pulling from the past, searching for the beaten paths that have paved the road for humanity's existence in the here and now, and sometimes, foreshadowing things to come.

In the complex world between fact and fiction, most of what follows is true.

As they came to be known, the Von Neumann self-replicating machine was hypothesized in a series of lectures at the University of Illinois in 1949. The question of complexity was the driver of these thought experiments. John von Neumann wanted to know not just how complex a machine had to be to replicate itself but also how complicated it had to be to evolve.

As we now understand, complexity is also at the heart of information theory. Andrey Kolmogorov was interested in writing the shortest possible computer programs to produce a product. Kolmogorov Complexity was introduced in 1963 and can best be described as the measure of computational resources needed to fulfill an algorithm.

Decades later, Physicist Vahe Gurzadyan showed that the complexity of the human genome was relatively low and could easily be transmitted by radio waves. The concept of Information Panspermia was introduced in 2005. The thesis was groundbreaking enough to be cataloged as a possible answer to the Fermi Paradox.

The paper showed the ease at which the human genome could be sent; however, the question remained as to who would be on the other side to receive it.

CHAPTER ONE

THE WORLD

Amindful Tolver Farnaz plucked the newspaper out of the graffiti-tarnished dispensary to read the prominent headline, *Protest Turns Violent.*

Leafy edition after edition depicted a world growing more unsure of itself ever since government-backed scientists declared they had developed a way to travel back in time. The grand announcement exposed all the insecurities an uneasy global community could bear—battling rising sea levels, an ongoing nuclear disaster off the Sino-Eastern coast, and the post-pandemic failure of nation-states to unify on slowing the transmission of a deadly virus. Millions of people perished in its wake years after the virus had run its course, and still there was no consensus on the best way to defend against it. The newspaper would publish exhausting exposes every week on countries that had been pushed to the brink by one of these tragedies.

Outside of his purview, the world was on fire, and all Tolver could do was helplessly watch and read about it. He took in how these extreme regions glowed at night, boiled over with chaos during the day, and recoiled at how the leaders of these nation states pumped the population with lasting animosity for their adversaries. There were more and more regions where hate had been invited to grab the steering wheel and drive the populace headlong into the shadowy pits of humanity. He couldn't imagine himself stepping into any one of those areas unless he wanted to become another smudged spot on a field filled with craters, rubble, and other assorted wreckage commonly associated with violent human behavior.

Time and again, he told himself to stop reading about the insanity, to block out everything wrong with the world, but he just couldn't quit it, not with the unsettling possibilities that time travel presented. Tolver took in the pages of a newspaper, immersing himself in print, an investigator looking for the tell-tale signs of abuse by that technology.

He was starving for this type of mental engagement because he was having a difficult time accepting the role society wanted him to play. He lived in a modest fortified apartment in the middle of a neighborhood rife with an assortment of knuckle dragging thugs. Almost every neighborhood within the city was like this, with vandals and gangs waking up to rule the night. His evenings were spent boarded up in a makeshift bunker he called home. There the ugly howls of discontent bellowed through the streets like the wind. He didn't own a car because he knew it would only be pried open for parts. The vehicles left on the street were battered and broken, punching bags to a middle-class system that could no longer stay afloat.

When Tolver wasn't sealed up at home, he was working at Sand to Silicon, a company responsible for validating the authenticity of computer chips—an industry littered with counterfeits. Sand to Silicon was building a reputation as an outsourcing company for high-tech firms.

They acted as a stopgap to the orders those companies had placed for these valuable commodities. The chips were supposed to be layered, shaved from electro-grade silicon ingots and built one tier at a time to produce a flat, clean product. Its engineered ceramic innards measured in nanometers. The counterfeits that cluttered the market came close, but those thieves were only trying to replicate these parameters because of the massive amount of money waiting to be raked in after delivering these trojans. Tolver went about inspecting each chip using a high-intensity microscope to look for discolorations, dents, or burn marks that would indicate the product was tampered with or a forgery. Hundreds of thousands of these silicate wafers were delivered in neatly stacked bins to be inspected by the company every year. Often the bins took up so much floor space the employees created their own intricate maze of pathways to get around. Tolver dutifully reported to work. There were days he wandered between the bins as if he were a zombie trapped in the Capuchin Catacombs.

If he was in search of happiness, it was going to happen outside of his job. He found it far easier, and it required much less effort at the end of his week to sit at his local pub, have a beer, and give a go at having a substantive conversation.

As he discovered on more than one occasion, those meaningful discussions were difficult to keep afloat. Someone was destined to sink them with a juvenile retort, resolve a point by blaming a particular nationality, or cuss just because they had run out of something clever to say.

These were the calculated chances Tolver took while holding a newspaper and walking into his local watering hole.

At midday, this gloomy establishment was cast with its usual set of regulars, and his good friend Rowen. He could tolerate most of the others like he tolerated the pungent cloud that hung over the place from the night before. The swill of leftover alcohol and piss mixed in with cleaning fluids gave the bar a nauseating locker room stench that lingered in his nostrils until he could wash the adhering hit away with a beer. This was the cleanest watering hole within walking distance of his place that wasn't overrun by drug dealers and arrangements of a more shadier nature. Blake, the bartender, was the first to greet Tolver, followed by a few customers raising their glasses in a halfhearted salute while murmuring his name.

Approaching them at the far end, one of the regulars went a little further in acknowledging Tolver as he got closer, "Hey, it's about time you showed up with my crossword."

Tolver made sure the bar was dry before placing his paper down and leafing through to pull out the Entertainment and Puzzles section, "You know, Edwin, it wouldn't hurt if you bought a paper now and then."

"I don't want to read anything that rag has printed. I only want the crossword puzzle."

Rowen was already seated at the bar and didn't mind chiming in when it came time to speak out against Edwin. "He doesn't appreciate the paper's liberal overtones."

"I don't. It's a lot of horse manure."

It didn't take long for everyone to burst into laughter and mock poor Edwin. All were involved except for Blake and Tolver.

Rowen wouldn't let it die. He enjoyed sparring with Edwin. "And your party has brought us nothing but unemployment, sending jobs overseas and wrecking any semblance of the middle class. None of us need to read that in any paper when we all have to live it."

"Only because we have spent the last decade cleaning up the mess your president and his administration left us ..."

A chorus of boos greeted Edwin once again, but their chiding did little to silence him. "There are only so many giveaways, so much free stuff we can bestow upon a generation. But eventually, someone has to pay for this liberal extravaganza. All citizens, all of society, must eventually pay. I am sorry if you don't see that, but the bills have been piling up for some time and are now overdue."

Edwin grabbed the paper as it was passed to him and went to the crossword section, folding it to frame the puzzle so it was the only thing he would see.

Dissatisfied with Edwin's retort, Tolver grumbled, "That's not how government works."

Edwin never looked up from his puzzle. "You haven't a clue. That is *exactly* how government works."

There was some grumbling between the patrons

before Rowen spoke in a loud, clear voice, "Larceny."

They all turned to look at Rowen. Edwin peered up from the puzzle to see Rowen staring straight at him. "What?"

"You have no problem taking the crossword puzzle from my friend's paper ..."

"His newspaper?"

"Don't go there. Of course, he didn't print it or write the words, but he paid for it, and you take the crossword from him every chance you get."

"Because I have asked for it, and he has given it to me in the past. Should I wait for him to dump it in the garbage before rummaging through to find the crossword section?"

"No, but to even things out, you could have bought the paper every once in a while and given him the sections you weren't going to read."

"Why would I do that? We would both show up with a newspaper. I know he's always going to buy one, so why not share it?"

Rowen gave him a quizzical look, "Edwin, you said it yourself. At some point, the free ends, and every citizen should pay. That includes you!"

The bar burst into laughter, and Edwin stood up, fuming. He did not like having his words thrown back at him in this way. He reached deep into his pockets to pull out some cash, "But unlike your kind ... pay I will."

He threw the bills at Tolver, but Rowen wasn't ready to let the subject go, "That may have paid for your use of the paper, but it comes nowhere near covering this man's time. After all, he is the one who is making his way to the newspaper stand. He is the one who hand-delivers the crossword puzzle to you."

Edwin glared at Rowen with a beet-red face that got brighter by the second. The veins in his neck and head were beginning to bulge, "Not one penny more!"

It was all he could say before storming out of the bar and through the back door, crossword puzzle in hand. He did not hear the jeers and cheers of those he left behind.

"Now you've done it, Rowen. Chasing my patrons from the bar, that will be enough out of you today," Blake said half-jokingly as he walked over and picked up Edwin's abandoned beer.

"He'll be back, Blake." Unfortunately for Rowen, the sentiment was weak and backed up by a rather smug smile.

"I expect you to pick up his share until his return since we are calling in all accounts due," Blake's eyebrow shot upward. "The man is good for a few belts after his beer, and you chased him away before he was finished with his first round of suds."

Rowen reached about the bar, picking up the money thrown at Tolver, and handed it to Blake.

"What's this?" Blake looked incredulous.

"The difference you are asking for while Edwin is away...unless, of course, you feel it's not enough."

"That's not your money to give. That's his money." Blake's thumb made an overt gesture in Tolver's direction.

"I'm sure Tolver doesn't mind."

"And I'm pretty sure he does. You need to come up with your own cash to satisfy this situation; that's a fact."

"It's alright, Blake," Tolver interrupted. "Rowen can use the cash to pay the bill."

Rowen slapped the bar, celebrating the decision, "You see, you big mucker, I told you so."

"I should throw the both of you out. The two of you drive me crazy."

"Wait a minute. Are you saying I drive you crazy?" Tolver shot back, obviously offended. "I didn't say a thing. It was the two of them."

"No, it's you as well. Trust me."

Rowen and the others in the bar got a good chuckle at how Tolver had gotten dragged into the argument.

"Me? How can you say that?"

"You have sat on that barstool quite a few times, telling us how you have given to people in their moment of need."

There was a pause as they waited for Blake to finish his line of thought when he suddenly blurted out, "Well, you agree with that statement, right?"

"Damn straight," Tolver said proudly as the other patrons nodded in agreement.

"You've told us more than once that you have gone out of your way to buy a bum a warm meal, like a steak sandwich, so go on and tell us again—why?"

Tolver felt a little uneasy regaling them with his deeds on this subject but acts of kindness were a part of who he was, and he certainly didn't feel ashamed of it. "Well, I am hoping that when they bite into something like a warm pretzel bun and taste the grilled steak within, the crisp green lettuce and spicy deli mustard, it takes them back to a moment in their life when eating like that was commonplace. I'm hoping that it gives them something to fight for."

"And right now, you don't feel the money that was thrown at you is something to fight for? It was yours as soon as it was given to you; you never even had to pick it up. The people in here already recognized those were your bills. Seriously, if you don't stand up for yourself in those instances, then how the hell can you expect a total stranger to do what you want in fighting for a memory of eating something like a steak sandwich?"

Rowen reached over and jabbed Tolver on the shoulder, "I'm afraid he's got you there, partner."

"... and agreeing with me won't get you out of what you owe." Blake shook a finger at Rowen as a reminder for driving Edwin away. He turned his back on the both of them and walked to the other end of the bar to do some work that eventually led to the storeroom.

"Money isn't everything," Tolver muttered just loud enough for Rowen to hear.

"I don't know about that. Look at the front page and tell me that's not about money." Rowen tapped the headline of the paper.

"Protest turns violent ... it's not about money; that's about the government's time travel program."

"Don't kid yourself. It's one and the same thing."

"How do you figure? These people are scared, worked up by the misinformation that is being put out there. They think the government is altering our future."

One of the other patrons chimed in, "If I had a time machine, I know exactly what I would do. I would go back to my high school and ask Susan Harmotto to the prom."

They all chuckled as one of them belched at the suggestion. It caused others to fire out wildly insane ideas. "I would go back and bet on one of the Super Bowls, find a year where a big upset took place, and put all my money on the winning team."

"To hell with that. I would go back and find my younger self, tell him how to invest in the companies that are destined to make it big."

Rowen grabbed his drink and smiled broadly, "I told you, Tolver. You see? It's all about the money."

"I don't see it like that. For the people who get all

worked up over this, it's about ideology. It's about who is controlling this thing. They think the government will use the technology to take total control. To push their agenda," Tolver insisted.

"Well, those who are established have power, and that power probably comes from them being around a lot of money," said Rowen.

"The people protesting aren't the ones in power. They are just like you and me, only they're frightened, and it's not about money or control. It's about what they have to lose."

"You don't know that. You certainly don't know if they are like you and me. Let me tell you, if they were, they wouldn't be out there protesting. They would be in a bar grabbing a drink."

"No, that's not altogether true. In fact, I think it's quite the opposite. If we felt pressured as they do, then we would be out there just the same, and after some of the things we have seen recently, we should be protesting with them."

"Protesting what? You think time travel is creating all this chaos, pushing us into all these conflicts?"

"No, no, I don't. I think the patience of a lot of people is being stretched in ways that leave them feeling hopeless and no longer in control. Recent events don't help. Reports are coming out from areas in the world of elected officials who looked to have no chance of winning but have now been voted into office; of sporting events with teams who are the underdogs going into their season but win it all in the end, and of internal conflicts where a small uprising appears as if it has no chance and is going to fail but then suddenly, is victorious. These incidents no longer look like a stroke of luck or someone beating the odds; it looks to be the blatant interference by the government, and that perception, right or wrong, is what drives a lot of proponents against this technology."

Rowen brought the glass of beer toward his lips for another swig and, before taking it, blurted out a thought meant to be light-hearted, "Well, if anything, it gives people someone to blame for things that are out of the ordinary."

Tolver raised his eyebrow and tapped the headline in the newspaper to emphasize his point, "Go on, joke about it, but for some, blame isn't enough. Some are more radical in their approach, resorting to acts of vandalism, violence, and if all else fails, have started to participate in acts of terror."

Rowen was in mid-gulp. Tolver could see his wheels turning and knew he wouldn't stop drinking until he nailed down a reply. It wasn't until he finished his pint, belched in satisfaction, and set down the empty glass just hard enough to get the bartender's attention that an almost sinister grin appeared on Rowen's face.

The wicked smile caught Tolver off guard, "And why are you smirking at me like that?"

Another of the patrons remarked at Rowen when they saw this, "Jeez, he looks like the cat that ate the freaking canary. What gives, man?"

Rowen nodded in agreement with this patron's assessment and pointed emphatically at Tolver, "You see, I know something this dunderhead doesn't. He can get as high and mighty as he wants about defending these protestors, but when all is said and done, he'll be right there, just like the emphatic supporters of this technology, pushing it on the population and telling us there is nothing to fear."

"What are you talking about?" Tolver set his paper aside, genuinely stumped by Rowen's last remark.

"I know you, man. I know you far better than you think I know you. Once you experience something like this, you won't be so against it."

"Wait a minute, what have you done?"

"There is a commercial side to this time travel, and it's been described by many as being surreal, sublime, mind-blowing ... a real life-changing experience."

"Rowen, don't mess with me right now. You know there is nothing more I would like than to immerse myself in this technology and experience it firsthand." Tolver grew wide-eyed as he spoke. The patrons in the bar could feel the mounting energy grow as Rowen went in for the kill.

"I know! That's why me and the fellas have chipped in and got you a slot with the only premier commercial time travel company around. This shit isn't cheap; but somehow, we got ourselves all a spot." Rowen reached for the freshly poured beer Blake placed in front of him, immediately put three fingers into the glass and scooped out a large swatch of foam. "Damnit, Blake, how many times have I told you I hate foam in my beer?" Rowen flicked it onto the floor as a few patrons laughed out loud and cheered at this rebellious act.

"It helps keep the flavor in," Blake said indignantly. "Foam acts as an insulator."

Rowen held his beer up for Blake to see. "I'm drinking a domestic tap beer. How much flavor can there be?"

Tolver jumped off his barstool and grabbed Rowen by his shoulders. Rowen quickly shifted his beer to the side as more suds and foam spilled out. Tolver wouldn't let go. "Hey, to hell with the flavor. Finish what you were saying. When are we going?"

Rowen held his glass, waiting for the sloshing of the beverage to settle before he calmly set it back on the bar, "Sooner than you might expect, and you'll never guess who put in the lion's share of the funds ... Nathan!"

"Nathan? I don't understand. Did he hit it big on the ponies?"

"I guess he was very determined to do it. Paid for most of it himself. I say it's about time that cheap bastard paid for a round of something, wouldn't you agree? Anyway, happy early birthday, buddy. You, me, Slater, and Nathan are going to experience everything Tilt Time has to offer."

CHAPTER TWO

ENTANGLEMENT ENGINEERS

J ulianne Bobrick had been unwittingly grooming for destiny ever since entering the master's program for mathematics back at Harvard. Her cutting-edge papers on quantum mechanics—specifically in Spectral Theory and Quantum Spin Systems—caught the eye of her professors. Her credentials were passed on to the Belfer Center for Science and International Affairs, a top-notch think-tank linked to Harvard. Here, the best minds in the country gathered to solve the toughest problems facing not only the nation but the world. She was surreptitiously ushered to a team of scientists involved in a confidential program referred to as the Information Field Project. It was described to her as a highly technical campaign designed to locate time travel anchor points smattered about the globe.

Julianne's team was front-and-center in the hunt for entangled particles, but not just any web of atoms joining together. They were after the newly confirmed axion particles. Finding axions meant one was in contact with the substance of space, or more specifically, with dark matter. Of all the energies and particles in existence, dark matter was what filled the skies. She was told that if they could find axions, then they had a chance of locating its partner, the even more elusive graviton. It was proven that axions and gravitons became entangled, just like electrons and photons. The only difference was when a graviton became embedded in a heavy mineral—like iron ore, rutile, zircon, granite, or even something as simple as steel—it couldn't move at the speed of light like a photon flying through space, which made them much easier to find.

Massive amounts of computing power were harnessed to design tools and instruments to detect these entangled particles. For whatever the reason, the emphasis was placed on unearthing gravitons. A whole new branch of specialists known as entanglement engineers were rapidly trained and cut loose to chart these quantum nodal points that clung to the globe.

The instant the time travel program became operational, Julianne and her co-workers were sent to locations like the Badlands National Park, where dinosaur fossils were found in troves, to Dealey Plaza, where John F. Kennedy was assassinated. or Fort McHenry in Baltimore. The fort withstood an assault by British forces in mid-September 1814 and was where Francis Scott Key got his inspiration for the Star-Spangled Banner. With their successes, the list of historical sites grew exponentially.

However, if they wanted to send someone back to Antiquity, the Dark Ages, the Russian Empire to witness the reign of the Tsars or the Ashikaga Shogunate period where the kamikaze winds saved Japan from a Mongol invasion, they would need permission from the foreign government ruling over those territories. Once on-site, an entanglement engineer would capture the essence of an entangled anchor point in a specialized collector and take it back to Brookhaven National Laboratory in Upton, New York. The Relativistic Heavy Ion Collider had gone right past its

Electron Ion upgrade and had become an extension of the information field generator.

Initially, this quantum computer was there to assist the physicists at the institute with their work in identifying the particles that flew off these high-speed collisions. Its goal was to unlock more efficient ways to develop energy. And develop it did. The qubit field inside this quantum computer, like every quantum computer, was based on the sensitive man-made science of entanglement.

The process of entanglement in nature happened as easily as hydrogen and oxygen bonding to create water. On the other hand, artificial entanglement was a fragile endeavor that needed to be shielded from outside interference and left undisturbed. Through the layers of isolation, the blue and yellow concentric rings of the Relativistic Heavy Ion Collider was one of the first ways the quantum computer had gained contact with the world. In doing so, the information field did everything in its power to make these rings more efficient. These improvements were what finally gave way to the information field generator discovering new and exotic ways to bend time. However, a quantum computer didn't function like a typical classical computer one found on their desk. A person couldn't use a quantum computer as a word processor, check emails, or interact on social media. This robust yet delicate machine would spit out math-based answers that needed to be interpreted by its human counterparts. Sifting through these piles of numbers was like brushing away the mounds of sand at an archeological site, only in this instance the equations revealed artifacts that would come to be known as the entanglement corridors.

A type of excitement ensued within the scientific community that hadn't been seen in generations. As the official word spread for sending people back in time, most countries found themselves willing participants, allowing the entanglement engineers entry. What wasn't clear was what steps the program would take with countries that weren't so open to the process. The company line was that the sovereignty of each nation would be respected, whether they were a participant in the program or not. There were plenty of reasons a country might not want to know what happened in their past. This kind of historic revelation might question the rule of a regime, revive territorial disputes, or even shake the foundations of religious beliefs.

Despite the concerns of these opposing nations, those in charge felt it necessary to get as complete a picture of the human condition as possible, not just for the record but to survive the future. In order to do that, the government needed access to every historic venue on the planet, whether a country was willing to cooperate or not.

Julianne experienced firsthand what it took to be at that campus. Beyond the educational requirements needed to work at Brookhaven, one had to pass an interview and background check. When those in charge were going through the files of their entanglement engineers, Julianne's exceeded all their expectations. She was asked to join a concealed sector of the operation that specialized in collecting particles in hostile areas abroad. This concealed sector was known as the Special Collections Branch. The SCB was the clandestine arm of the time travel program. It had her upgrading her clearance beyond top-secret, giving her a pass to areas within Brookhaven that others on campus were denied.

Julianne's new job would have her flying into a neighboring country or province under a cover, such as an archaeologist, a geologist, or even an aid worker. She would contact covert operatives that would set her up with local friendlies or guides to get her into those restricted borders. Once in country, she would collect the particle and make a hasty retreat. To say it was exciting work was an understatement; it was an adrenaline rush to which she found herself addicted.

She continued accepting missions, continued seeking assignments, and continued wondering how far she could push things before it all went wrong.

CHAPTER THREE

TERRA D' ANDORRA

I n 1954, the Tokyo (Haneda) International Airport was the hub for a country rebounding from the last world war. There was an inherent enthusiasm for investing in an economy that could do nothing but grow. Companies swung their doors open wide to the daily inrush of foreign investors. Once one reached the island, there was a flurry of activity, hitting the ground running with purpose and taking advantage of the wheeling and dealing that was interminably present within this atmosphere. These buyers and sellers knew no ceiling and freely colluded to rebuild the economy with nothing but an abundance of profits in mind.

Haneda was a gateway for this enthusiasm. After arriving on the tarmac, businessmen were funneled around the construction of the main terminal and the soon-to-be-completed modern control tower. This advanced terminal would accommodate the influx of people to this booming economy and give much-needed support to their carrier, Japan Air Lines (JAL), with its new license to fly international routes. This construction was also crucial because the current carriers shared the airfield with the United States Air Force. Upon completion, these carriers would turn over the old terminal to the military for their exclusive use.

To keep up with the airport's commercial expansion, the government hired individuals to cover baggage handling, ticket sales, aviation mechanics, terminal maintenance, security, and administrative needs.

In mid-July, a gentleman approached the customs counter looking like any of the businessmen in his formal dark suit, Stetson hat, a tie that transitioned from gray to black, and Clubmaster sunglasses. He carried a briefcase and, when it was appropriate, presented his passport to the official. As the agent took the document, he asked where the man was from, and the man responded that he was from Taured. When asked again, the gentleman stated quite clearly as being from Taured. The envoy hailed another customs agent to look at the passport and listen in. After being asked for the third time and responding in kind, the officers could sense the man was becoming agitated and asked him to obligingly step into a room they had reserved for the further questioning of travelers.

A supervisor showed up with security detail, and the manager instructed the guards to stand outside the door. The supervisor then made his way in, saw an individual seated on the other side of the desk. The supervisor began leafing through the passport. He asked the man to place his personal items on the counter. The supervisor looked over the man from Taured as he went about collecting the things from his pockets. Upon closer inspection, the man from Taured appeared to be beaten up—he had a split lip, numerous abrasions on his face, and a bruised wrist that was exposed as he produced things like his identification. These injuries were by no means fresh but seemed to indicate an ongoing struggle. The supervisor examined the stamps on his passport pages, which showed the man in question regularly traveled throughout Europe and Japan several times over the past few years. This revelation caused the supervisor to raise an eyebrow, and he glanced down to see what personal items the man had produced. There were recognizable European currencies of all types, house keys on a small ring, tickets for his flight and baggage claim, and a wallet. The supervisor asked the man again where he was from, and in response, the man once again stated that he was from Taured. The supervisor shook his head and raised his hand to stop the individual from saying anything else. He stated point-blank that no such country existed. The man became heated and retorted that Taured had been in existence for quite some time.

The supervisor ordered that the chart be drawn down. An agent pulled a string, and a map of the world revealed itself as it descended from the encased roller hung high above and behind the desk. The supervisor motioned for the man to get up and show him where Taured was. The man got up and looked the map over carefully.

"I cannot show you where Taured is."

"And why not?"

"Because this map is inaccurate. It's been drawn up after the war, and the country has been omitted."

The supervisor insisted he show them, but the man refused, saying he would not participate in such a folly. The supervisor got up and pointed to the map asking again for the man to identify the area.

"Then, you're pointing at it now."

The area the supervisor had pointed to was the principality of Andorra between France and Spain, tucked away in the Pyrenees mountains. The supervisor stated what was clearly written on the map.

"That is Andorra. There is no Taured."

The man became heated and stated that of course it must be Andorra. They printed a map without Taured on it. He insisted there was no way for Taured not to exist. He went on murmuring angrily about being tested in this way and treated in such a catechized and rude fashion.

Seeing how agitated this traveler was becoming, the supervisor changed the subject and asked what business the international traveler had in Japan. The man eventually calmed down and stopped ranting. He searched through his briefcase until he produced paperwork that looked to be from the Nikon company. It stated he was there to negotiate a possible contract for French Algeria. The man from Taured, regaining his composure, explained that Algeria was under a lot of pressure to launch their television station the following year, so he was in the process of trying to close a deal. The customs supervisor didn't like the way the explanation sounded. Picking up the phone, he called the Nikon company. He spoke at some length before concluding that the company had no record of any dealings with this foreigner.

The man from Taured was incensed and claimed he had been misrepresented as being an employee of the Nikon company when he was, in fact, a negotiator for the French Algeria communications board. The supervisor wasn't about to pick up the phone and call them back on this one technicality, so he heard the man out. As the man claiming to represent the French Algerian television division spoke, he became confused. He chewed on his thumbnail, nervously looked around, and muttered about possibly not having done things in the right order.

When he became quieter and calmed down, the supervisor ordered the agent to put the contents from the man's pockets inside a large Manila envelope. The papers were returned to the briefcase, and it was all placed in a box that the supervisor would later secure in his office.

He then explained to the man from Taured that he was to be taken to the Hilltop Hotel in Tokyo without his passport. He was informed the customs department would place guards at his door, and he was asked not to leave under any circumstances. For this reason, if he needed something to eat, toiletries, or any other necessities, he was to use the hotel's room service. In the meantime, his case would move through the appropriate channels, and the proper officials would contact him the following day. It would be then that they would make another attempt at sorting this mess out. Reluctantly, the man from Taured agreed to these terms and retired to the Hilltop Hotel with guards in tow.

The following morning, after knocking several times and trying to hail their mysterious guest, the guards summoned the hotel staff to open the door. When they were finally able to get in, they found the room empty. The furniture and items inside were untouched, and the bed had not been disturbed.

Back at the airport, the supervisor discovered that the box containing the man from Taured's personal property was now empty. All of his belongings, including his passport, were gone.

The local newspapers mentioned that the authorities were trying to track this unknown traveler down, but it was to no avail and never solved.

It was as if the man from Taured had never existed.

CHAPTER FOUR

KASHMIR

Nathan Daugherty looked at himself in the mirror and had to laugh. The guys down at the Boomerang Room had been giving him a hard time about his long, thick sideburns and matching mustache. They said it made him look like a pimp, but those kinds of remarks didn't rub him the wrong way—and truth be told, he loved the attention he was getting because of it. His lack of concern for their remarks had more to do with why he was growing out his facial hair than any particular look he was cultivating for their amusement. Sure, those guys were right about him resembling a pimp, which was why he was able to laugh at himself now. But what this look could gain him was worth more than any embarrassment from the guys back at the strip club. If the plan he was hatching worked, he would get the last laugh.

He began putting together his scheme the instant he acknowledged he was in a serious rut. He considered himself employed, but no one in his circle took his being a full-time gambler seriously. How could they know he was hooked on the craft ever since he flipped for his first baseball card back in grade school? All he could think about was where his next game of chance might crop up. Gambling triggered something inside him, something primordial within his being. It burned like a torch, sucking up the air for any other interest he might have had. This combustible light became the driving force in his life. For every gambler, no matter what the challenge, this eventually translated into hustling a mark.

As he grew older, it seemed that life was all about the hustle, about getting the one up on someone. This may have been why he never felt comfortable with a regular job, not with the riches from the success of others being ostentatiously flaunted about. In his eyes, the government held a person down from ever attaining that kind of success. The powers that be had their clutches on the wallet of every person punching the clock. Those workers were suckers; they would never get ahead in life—not that way. The man had it all figured out and based it on something as simple as the hours on a timecard.

For as far back as Nathan could remember, the government had a monopoly on time. It was extremely odd that a thing happening naturally—and long before mankind ever existed—suddenly needed to be regulated by an administrative authority. No matter where one looked, the government was there trying to piece the puzzle of time together. They had employees maintaining fossil records, weighing in on the Planck scale of the quanta, and reaching out beyond the visible horizon of the universe to measure the accuracy of cosmological theories. They did all of this from a planet floating far from the center of the universe. They divided their blue pearl with lines of longitude and latitude and divided their nations into Eastern, Central, and Pacific time zones. They standardized the hourly wage and taxes and developed an atomic clock to keep all those ticking seconds marching in uniform like little tin soldiers. With the development of time travel, the government was now putting a lock on who could participate in the activity and when.

Knowing that not everyone could financially spring for the experience hounded Nathan. It was like buying a ticket to be launched into space—only here, a tourist wasn't stuck in a tin can wearing a space suit; the participant was able to experience what the past had to offer. He drank in every blog and report about anyone with information, hoping to get a glimpse beyond the public dealings of Tilt Time. He avidly followed news feeds about the company, and as he got more comfortable with the feedback, he began contemplating the possibilities of staying there and forming a new life if he decided to travel back.

The day the literature for Tilt Time hit his mailbox, he hungrily poured over its pages in search of the right opportunity. The packages they offered potential customers were diverse and expansive. They focused on immersing the participants in the entertainment value of where they were traveling as opposed to going on something benign, like a bird-watching excursion or a scientific expedition. As far as Nathan was concerned, participation was a good thing, for it meant everything was in play, and he liked his chances of getting lost in the moment. He remembered exhaling long and hard when the price tag came in. His cheeks had filled with air till they hurt, but as he exhaled, he slowly built up the courage to obtain the money for this excursion. Raising this kind of dough wasn't going to be easy, and if the past was any pretense to his future, he wouldn't win it by laying it down on the ponies or flipping for it with baseball cards.

With thoughts of a new beginning playing in his head like a needle that had been dropped on a rock album long ago, he internally embraced his pimp look as he coolly strolled over to see Paulie Polizzi. Nathan hardly dressed the part, wearing one of his usual faded collared shirts. It had more wrinkles than a *tele-novella,* and the slacks he wore weren't that far behind in needing a press. His brown shoes were so scuffed they looked more like a pair of moccasins than anything even remotely close to being off the rack at Florsheim. Though this wasn't far from how he usually dressed, he had explicitly cultivated this look to ask Paulie for a favor.

Paulie was better known in the neighborhood as the Shark. Paulie was a guy who loaned money, and many assumed that's how he got his nickname, but that wasn't true. It's what happened to a person who didn't repay one of those loans that earned Paulie his nickname. Early in his career, Paulie tore into one guy so badly down by the pier that the crime scene investigators thought the victim had been attacked by a shark.

Nathan strolled over to Paulie's inner sanctum, an established bar in the neighborhood called Calabella's. It was cash-only, with bottled beers and the standard fare of hard liquor to properly pickle one's liver. Besides watching one of the two television sets, one could play tunes on the jukebox, throw darts, or pick up a game at one of the two pool tables. It was easy to pick up a game because there was always someone in there looking to hustle a sucker. These were the distractions to the real action taking place in the back, where Paulie took care of business. Within the four walls of that room, one could put down a wager on a contested match or an upcoming fight, or one could take it to the next level and borrow money from Paulie to place on a game of chance.

Nathan cut through a light haze as he made his way over the small warps of the floor of the near-empty bar and toward the back room. There were always a couple of heavies hanging out at the entrance to the office. Dressed like two regulars, they were there to stop anyone from approaching Paulie. It was probably because they did everything by word of mouth under this roof. There wasn't a phone you could call Paulie on—the man was insulated.

The bouncers were the messengers, relaying to Paulie what each visitor wanted. If Paulie didn't like what he heard or the way a guy looked, he had them dismissed, but if the proposition sounded interesting, then Paulie would wave them in. Nathan was held up at the doorway briefly. Once Paulie recognized who had come calling, he was given a pass. He knew Nathan well enough from years of wagers to gauge why he might be there. This time, though, Paulie would be in for a surprise and might have regretted not vetting Nathan a little more thoroughly.

The drab room lacked any kind of congenial décor. Its dark walls were lined with various boxes of booze they used to stock the bar. It was thick with cigar smoke, the smell of cheap cologne, and sweat; there were no windows to escape this odoriferous masculine squalor. The oversized desk in the center of the room presented a bit of a puzzle for how they got it through the door. Paulie sat behind it, always going over receipts. One had to wonder if there were ever any receipts for the bar or was it all just money he had out on the street.

"Nate, come on in. What's cooking?" Paulie's voice was gruff, as if he had been yelling at the top of his lungs the day before.

"Hey, Paulie, I was rolling an idea around in my head, and I wanted to run something by you."

Paulie went back to looking at the stubs he had organized on his desk for upcoming weekend bets, "Lay it on me, kid."

"I was wondering if I could get a hold of a half-million dollars."

Paulie immediately pulled the handbrake on what he was doing. His jaw went slack as he looked up at Nathan with a stern, quizzical look, "What the hell did you just say to me?"

Nathan felt the lump in his throat forbid him from asking again, and rightly so, but he fought through it, "I was wondering if I could get a hold of a half-million dollars?"

"Hey, Bully, come in here."

One of the heavies left his post at the doorway and stood beside the desk, "What's up, boss?"

Paulie made Nathan repeat his question, "Can you believe the set of brass balls on this guy, Bully? He actually walked in here and asked me that question. The guy borrows a couple thousand here and there over the past couple of years, and you think that earns you the right to ask me a question like that?"

"Paulie, I wasn't trying to disrespect you. I just wanted to get front and center on an in over at the track."

"Horses, Nate? Really, that's what this is all about? You got some sort of sure thing, a banker? I can't believe I'm hearing this."

"Yeah, I got this in ... a buddy of mine is good friends with the clerk—"

"You got an in, a friend of a friend, the clerk of the course. I wish I had a dollar for every time I've heard that sitting here behind this desk. Everyone always has a sure thing until after the race, then it's, 'Paulie, the track was wet,' or 'It rained that day; how was I supposed to know?' 'Or Paulie, of all the dumb luck, the horse sprains his leg in the home stretch, they boxed him in, they pulled up,' or 'Paulie, they switched out the jockeys.' Then the sure thing is out the window, and everyone is looking at me for sympathy and a break, but I'm not the one who switched out the jockeys, and I sure as hell ain't the one who made it rain on race day. Here's the thing, when they need money, they know where my office is, but when they gotta pay me back, it's like I don't even exist on a map. Now, as sure as Sunday comes at the end of that first week when I haven't seen them, I gotta track them down and talk sense into them. I'm telling you right now, some of these welshers need to know a bullet is waiting for them before they get smart and motivated. I'd do it too Nate, just as if they were that horse that pulled up lame down the stretch back at the track. Believe me when I tell you I'd do it; these welshers are like lame horses. Now, I don't know what you got going on, but I'm trying to do you a favor. This is a fiscal upgrade in life, my friend. One that I don't think you would ever recover from if it didn't work out the way you hoped."

"Paulie, I hear what you're saying. I've thought this through. I mean, I was going to ask you for a million—"

Paulie let out a hearty laugh, which caused Bully to chuckle openly as well, "Jeez, Bully, do you hear this guy? He ain't listened to a word I said. What? You think you're giving me some kind of break by asking me for only *half*? Listen, Nate, that kind of money is not sitting around here hiding in one of these boxes. If I gotta get a half-million or a million, I gotta get on the horn and talk to some people. At a certain point, it's all the same work. It's phone calls, it's pickups. I gotta sit here and figure the terms, and then you gotta agree to them. And it's not you saying yes after I tell you; it's you being sent away to think this thing through, even if it's in the other room at the bar. Cause when you say yes to a deal like this, and it doesn't work out ..." Paulie cocked his head a little as he stared at Nathan, giving him the sternest of looks. "You won't get two nickels to rub together from anyone out on the street, but that will be the least of your problems cause those same two nickels might be the things the funeral home uses to cover up your eyes. You hear what I'm saying?"

"Paulie, I've thought about this, and I keep coming

back to the fact that if I pass on this opportunity, I'm going to be kicking myself for the rest of my life."

"You kicking yourself for the rest of your life is never going to come close to the beating you'll take if this thing goes south on you. *Capisce?* It's one thing to extend someone credit, but it's another to try to collect on it. In all my time doing this, I've never found being understanding as a solution to getting my money back. This isn't a process that is run on kindness or an extended payment plan. We are talking about a half-million here. There is a lot of discomfort and pain tied to this kind of money. Especially if what you're planning doesn't pan out."

"I know… I know."

Paulie was leaning back in his chair, with his hands on the edge of the desk, studying Nathan hard. His fat fingers moved about slowly as if he were playing the piano. After a few moments he leaned forward and tapped his cigar in an ashtray before placing it between his clenched teeth. "And you still want to go through with it? Bully, what are we going to do with our boy here?"

The question was greeted with silence, and the silence continued with neither party saying a word nor blinking an eye. Paulie finally broke the ice, "Alright, kid, I did my part. Let me make some phone calls. I'll get back to you with the terms. I just hope, for your sake, you can come through on them when it counts."

Paulie turned away to pick up the phone. Bully guided Nate toward the door. As he exited, Nathan couldn't hide his ear-to-ear grin as he obliged, even as thick wafts of cigar smoke mixed with the stale smell of cheap cologne followed them out.

CHAPTER FIVE

PACK STATIONS

He was minding his own business; at least, that's how he told it to whoever bothered to listen. Boone Masterson had to show plenty of concern for others while on the job, and so any social distancing he could achieve in his personal life was considered quality time. The campsite he had sought refuge was a usual get away along the backside of Yosemite National Park.

This was the place he camped and explored as a younger man during his stint at college, and so occasionally, he would return in search of that solace. He arrived at the pack station earlier that morning. He unloaded his rented, high-end sport utility vehicle and parked it in the shaded dirt lot for the duration of his stay. Along with the coolers, he had fishing gear, a duffle bag full of clothing, a couple of tents, tarps, rope, plenty of padding for the floor of his tent, and a large, comfortable sleeping bag. He kept most of these things when they weren't in use in a modest storage area down in the town of Bishop.

His camping supplies combined were more than a person could carry, especially since the campsite was several miles back into the mountains. The point of the pack station was to hire a mule. In fact, as many mules as one needed to carry their supplies to the destination. Boone had made his reservation well in advance to hold a spot. The people running the station knew the guests came here looking to get off the beaten path, so they placed them at one of the many secluded sites. This was precisely why Boone came calling time and again.

After dropping his gear off, he got the usual lowdown on how many other campers were in the area and how far they were relative to his site. They also informed him of any bears or other wildlife sightings that might affect his camping experience. Once he got the blessing from one of the guides, Boone threw on his camel pack, grabbed his small backpack containing his lunch, donned his sun hat and sunglasses, and began hiking up the wooded trail to the mountain pass. It was the middle of spring, and cool fresh air blew down from off the glacier caps high above. The bloom was in full swing, layering the hillsides, plains, and valleys in a thick coat of radiant reds, yellows, and purples. The bloom was doing so well that the colors were visible from the orbiting space stations high overhead.

He put his miles in, gradually making his way out of the valley and into the mountains, through patches of forest and past scenic vistas majestically rising up around him. Those snowcapped peaks and clear blue skies made it seem as if he was on another planet, far away from the steady flow of garbage and pollution that slowly piled up to swallow the world. Getting to the campsite in this way wasn't considered a steep climb by Boone—at least, not until he got to the last few hundred yards when he would have to get off the main trail and take a switchback. He couldn't help but notice on each of his outings that no matter how much he trained for this hike, those last few hundred yards always kicked his butt.

It was worth the effort. Boone had himself a small slice of paradise with a pristine lake, complete with gushing waterfalls from the snowmelt. During the day, the sound of the falls were straight out of a lush tropical rainforest, and by night, the soothing cascade would lull him into a deep, relaxing sleep. It was the perfect escape from his job—a job that never quit asking for just a little more out of him, pushing him ever closer to the edge of his physical and mental capacity.

After an assignment, there was always downtime as he would be on the mend. Having to recuperate on their supervised terms was more akin to being locked away in an asylum. Once checked in, they would lead Boone down a long corridor that flowed into an immense space where they had several large hyperbaric compartments masquerading as decontamination chambers.

With the facility being a few floors underground, there were no windows or any way for him to see the outside world, feel the warm rays of the sun or even hear a bird sing. His stays in those chambers were broken up into parcels of time marked by the random interviews of his medical overlords, ranging from topics of the management of his mission, techniques he used out in the field, and a steady evaluation of his mental health.

He was under constant scrutiny. They looked for inaccuracies, grilled him until they had squeezed every bit of information out of him, and when they were satisfied with his answers and deemed him fit, he was reinserted back into society. There were marshals in his precinct who found the constant badgering while locked away in a chamber to be downright obtrusive; they didn't understand why those in charge were doubting what these professionals had witnessed and experienced.

The doctors claimed they wanted a more antiseptic environment so that the patients had a better chance of healing. That's what they claimed, but this colorless, germ-free mandate seemed to be cold and calculating on their part. This lack of warmth pushed a person to their wit's end. The few things these patients were given in isolation, a deck of cards, coffee cups, a plastic chair, or an electronic tablet were all subjected to targeted abuse.

Boone related to the reports of individuals losing their minds and flipping out. He found himself on more than one occasion rocking himself back and forth in a chair within the dead quiet of a chamber. The blank white walls slowly closing in. Subjected to the crushing quiet as if he were sinking a thousand fathoms below the surface. Forced to look at the ghastly reflection of himself in the thick unbreakable observation glass. The bloodshot eyes. The snarl of gnashing teeth. The veins popping in his neck until the whole of him toppled over with uncontrollable rage. His bouts with losing it must have been mild compared to others. No orderlies were coming into his chamber because he kicked a chair across the room or scribbled graffiti on a wall. There were stories from others who had stayed in these antiseptic environments of fighting orderlies and physical restraint. Yet, for as often as Boone had been in one of those chambers, he never even saw a wrinkle in a sheet. It was so clean it could have easily passed for proof the previous person never existed.

And he existed. It was the reason he needed to get away from that center, and in his case, the seclusion of this mountain range could be considered therapeutic. No one could reach him out here; he was alone, on his terms, surrounded by the grandeur of nature, mountains of monumental stature, fresh air with hits of pine, pockets of petrichor, and patches of fragrant scented flora.

It was late in the afternoon when he arrived at his destination. Boone immediately went to work setting up his camp. He always had two tents—one for himself and one for the things he wanted to protect from inclement weather in case it should arise. In this elevation, a localized storm was never out of the question. To complete his setup, he stretched out and tied off two giant tarps over each tent to help protect them. This layering provided additional shade and kept things cool during the day, and if rain were to fall, the tarp was there to take the brunt instead of a downpour directly onto the tents.

By the time he had finished putting his campsite together, it was evening, and the sun had drifted behind the mountains. He used those last moments of light to gather a small amount of firewood. Stacking the timber in the pit, he struck a match and watched as the flames hungerly ate at the timber and fought to carve a niche in the advancing darkness. The fire signaled that dinner was the next thing on his adgenda. He planned on something simple straight out of a can. Chili, with a small bag of corn chips to be sprinkled when ready. The rest of his food for this trip was in a bear box he had rented back at the pack station, resting about a hundred feet away from where he had set up.

On occasion, he had discussions with colleagues who also enjoyed camping. It eventually revolved around food and what one ate while in the wilderness as opposed to what they ate at home. He had tried the same can of chili back at his house, and no matter how he prepared it, the spread always tasted like dog food. In the mountains, it was a different story. This same offering had the taste of being served at a five-star restaurant. They deduced it must have had something to do with being at altitude. He knew enough about physics to always buy his beer from a local brewer before making the final leg of the drive to the pack station. If the beer were kept near the same elevation, it would have the same amount of carbonation. Getting beer that was on a store shelf further away at a sea level and taking it to higher elevations affected the carbonation. When opened, it seemed almost fizzy due to all those tiny bubbles trying to escape. It was the reason he owned a T-shirt that read, *Support Your Local Brewer*.

After finishing dinner and cleaning up, he opened his second bottle of beer and got comfortable in his chair. He sat staring off into the night sky filled with a broad band of stars. The overlapping stellar group stretched out against the blackness of night, appearing as if they had been skillfully painted by an artist's hand. Besides the brightest star,

Cynosure, he didn't know too much about what was out there. Those points of light, that's where it all happened—that's how they were sending people back into time, or at least that's how it was explained to him. He didn't know about the inner workings of the information field generator, but then again, he didn't have to. It wasn't like he was running the damn place.

In that chair, gazing at the streaming patches of stars, he finally let his guard down and relaxed. The beer he was drinking, combined with fatigue and altitude, had the brew acting more like an eighty-proof malt scotch. The sound of the persistent deluge coming from the falls began to work its magic. The unending rhythm finally had him throwing the towel in and he got up, groggily stumbled into the tent, and climbed into his sleeping bag that was waiting to receive him.

The following morning, he awoke to the sounds of birds happily chirping. They buzzed around his tent, investigating the new structures, perching in places to make sure he didn't come out before they buzzed by the smoldering fire in search of crumbs. Boone lay there, imagining how he'd adjust the padding underneath his sleeping bag. He wasn't stiff, but he knew he could make it more comfortable. All the while the birds pecked away at what they could find.

After freshening up, he slipped into his usual routine of prepping his small backpack to include honey-based energy packets and put on his hydration-filled vest. Over that, he threw on his fishing vest and retrieved his rod and reel before donning his pack and heading off to higher elevations. The lake he was currently at—as well as some of the others nearby—were lakes everyone fished at. It wasn't as if the state stocked these waters. The fish here were wild. If he wanted something that might pass for dinner, he would have to hike deeper into the mountains to the ponds and watering holes at higher elevations.

This planned hike would represent the better part of his day, but if he happened to catch a fish when he made it to his destination, it would be the perfect way to cap off the day. He headed back down the switchback before crossing over to the main trail leading deeper into the wilderness. It was rumored if a person went far enough back and got up into the high plains, there was a herd of wild mustangs roaming about. Boone never made it that far on any of his travels but always had it on his bucket list of things to do. More often than not, the guides back at the pack station would take a person by horseback, so when they finally got there, one had a chance to ride alongside the untamed stallions and mares. He wanted to experience that at least once in his life.

Extended hikes like the one he was embarking on allowed him to let go, to put the grind behind him for a while, but they also served another purpose—secretly giving his body a run-through after being locked up in one of those chambers. The constant movement at altitude would break things down quickly and allow him to sense any soreness or discomfort within his joints or muscles. The thin air worked his lungs and heart so that if he became woozy or had sudden shortness of breath, he would immediately report the symptoms to the doctor at his next checkup. Boone thought it vital he stay on top of any signs of something going wrong inside his body. There were others in the program who might not have paid much attention to what was happening as they healed. He couldn't worry about how the other marshals handled their rehab. When it came to an imperfection, each marshal was on their own. Those back at his precinct were always challenging each other, playing handball, racquetball, or pickup games of basketball. They could have been doing this to test themselves, but that was the last way Boone wanted to find out he had a problem. Not with how some of those individuals waited before reporting anything. They talked themselves into letting their joints become aggravated or for unnatural bruising to appear. A few always waited until mission day before mentioning their problems to the medical staff. Maybe it was because the doctors constantly promised a traveler they would be in better shape upon their return. As far as Boone was concerned, he had put too much of himself into the program to leave anything to chance.

The trailhead had a canopy of trees lining the path to shade him from the late morning sun, giving the slopes and tree trunks a grated dappled look as he made his ascent. This serene view was accentuated by the occasional light wind and rustling of leaves, and in those moments, it seemed—if one wished hard enough—that the forest would reveal some of its magic. However, there wasn't much the forest could conjure up in that moment to stop his determination of testing himself by getting to a higher altitude. As this changeover happened for him, the air became cooler and thinner, causing him to breathe deeper as he made his push. The path beneath his feet had gone from the dark rich soil bordered by grass to a fine gray gravel. If one wasn't careful, they could slide right off in certain spots, which meant an unwanted trip to the bottom of the canyon. That was a fate no one would recover from, so he paid close attention to each step he took. This didn't mean he slowed his pace, but he was more mindful of how he navigated the trail. Being so focused, it was a minor miracle that he noticed the woman several yards down a slope, leaning against a fallen tree.

Boone froze for a moment as he processed the situation before asking if she was alright. She was doing her best to play off what had happened to her, but it was a poor performance, and he could tell by the crackle in her voice that she was in trouble.

"Let me come down and help you."

"That won't be necessary. I can make my way back up the grade," she replied.

Boone watched. When she made no attempt to leave the fallen tree, he retorted, "Is this attempt going to happen sometime today, or should I come back tomorrow when you finally decide to give it a go?"

"Very funny. I came down here because I thought I saw a branch I could fashion into a walking stick. I twisted my ankle coming down the trail earlier today and then got myself into this unfortunate circumstance."

He peeled the backpack from his shoulders and set it aside on the ground, "I'm coming down to give you a hand."

"This is embarrassing."

"No, embarrassing would be you passing on the help and being stuck down there for the rest of the day."

She was tentative about his approach. Being vulnerable and flustered by her predicament wasn't helping, but seeing his sincerity soon had her surrendering to his offer. It took effort on both their parts, but they worked their way back up to the path. Boone could see the toll the effort had taken in getting her back onto the trail. Her injury looked to be more severe than she had let on, and he ended up helping her all the way back to his campsite. On their return, he discovered she had been hiking for a few weeks, making her way across the Pacific Crest Trail. It was something she had been doing in sections over the past couple of years.

It was late in the afternoon, and it didn't take long for Boone to deduce that she was in no condition to continue her journey, so he invited her to stay, which she graciously accepted. It was a surprising move on both their parts, and the surprises would continue to unfold long after they had gotten to know each other.

CHAPTER SIX

THE ASSIGNMENT

There were strange noises bellowing from within the catacombs of the Brookhaven National Laboratory. Beyond the usual metallic pops and pings was the distant roar of thunder. Reportedly, the rumbling would echo out from the buried circular track accompanying the piping for the particle accelerator. At one time or another, those sounds were heard all over the campus. To a concerned public that caught wind of these events, it was explained away as a mass venting procedure, although as some internet sleuths pointed out, there were no giant exhaust fans on site. Some of the technicians wanted to blame the rolling pops and booms on the time machine. This was all well and good, but those turbulent eruptions happened even when the machine was idle, and so some came to the conclusion that the recent renovation of metallic hydrogen was to blame.

This metastable substance was one of the first major energy contributions the information field generator had bestowed upon mankind. Metallic hydrogen could be a fuel that made things like jets extremely fast, or rockets burn longer and sent farther than ever before into space. Metallic hydrogen could also be made into an extremely efficient superconductor. This new element was used in retrofitting the Relativistic Heavy Ion Collider, and because of this expansive upgrade it was rumored to be the most metallic hydrogen in any one place on the planet. Some technicians said because of this, the system was in flux, responding to its environment as if it were breathing, thus the loud roar of metallic thunder.

Working closely with the circular leviathan had the engineers injecting it with a personality as they brought their powerful invention to life. The technicians on site loved to gossip in this way, but the fact of the matter was the upgrade to the particle collider was what made the time machine possible. It got the program established and got people like Julianne Bobrick involved.

Thoughts about what went on in the lower chambers of Brookhaven would consume Julianne, especially as she would try to keep her mind off the dangers of her present situation. The sun had just dipped over the horizon as she made her way along a path filled with small stones and shale. This combination produced a surface that was as slick as ice. If she or one of her two armed guides slid off the path and into the ravine below it would lead to a very negative outcome. There was no way of telling if the person having fallen down the steep grade had survived, let alone find a way to retrieve them. Although she was told they were to be trusted, she was quite sure that if she slipped, her guides would leave her behind.

Julianne had worked her way deep into a territory that was forbidden for entanglement engineers—the reason she had gone undercover as an archeologist for the past few weeks—and now they were two klicks away from the rendezvous point where a next-generation stealth Black Hawk helicopter would take her back to base. From there, she would hitch a ride on one of the many military cargo jets going back to the States. She would be assured a seat on that flight because of what she possessed.

Getting her back to Brookhaven with the capsule intact was of the utmost importance. The capsule containing the particle had superconducting qualities driven by a laser inside—this technology suspended the particle, but the energy for this device did have its limits. The capsule was a very expensive egg timer, and when it reached zero, she would lose her work as well as the particle. They risked much on missions like this, searching for an anchor point in time.

As the twilight hour lingered, one of her guides requested they stop and wait for the cover of darkness. These moments were a nervous time for Julianne, but she reluctantly agreed. The constant threat of a rogue militant outfit finding them was both frustrating and terrifying at the same time, but there was little she could do. She waited just off the trail until her guides could make use of their night vision goggles which would allow them to continue.

She reached for her canteen and took a long drink of water, the cool offering hit the back of her parched throat. This might very well be the last time they took a break before reaching the chopper. She replaced the damp sweatband around her forehead with a fresh dry one and wiggled her toes in her hiking boots to feel for little pebbles or stones that might have worked their way under her arch. She was readying herself in the best possible way to make the last two klicks as easy as possible.

In the twilight of the desert, one of the guides

approached while she was busy performing these self-checks. It wasn't unusual to have them do this when they wanted to communicate. They didn't have radios and talking normally out in the open wasn't the smartest of ideas when trying to move undetected through the territory.

She was surprised by how well he spoke English, "I have worked with archeologists like you before and have seen them do what you did at the ruins. We both carefully watched as you attached the device you carry to one of the stones. I have always suspected that you leave something there, but when I checked, there were no indentations or holes. My friend over there thinks you took something. Could you please help us settle our disagreement?"

In the heat of that desert a chill spiked within her being. It caused her windpipe to contract, leaving little room to respond in the moment.

The guides were under strict orders not to question her about anything she was doing. They had been assigned to get her in and out undetected, yet here she was, being questioned in the middle of nowhere as darkness approached. The pressure to respond was mounting and she wondered if she didn't answer if she would make the rendezvous point on time. Julianne whispered as if she were in a church. Being as deliberate as she could with her answer, "I took a measurement of the ruin. We walked around it for a while before I did this to document where we were."

"Yes, but you needed to touch the ruin in only one place. No other time did you do this. How can it be a measurement of the whole?"

"I only needed to confirm the location of one stone. From there, we will use other measurements to recreate the structure."

"So, you are saying the device you carry can measure distances?"

"Something like that."

The man questioning her turned away and approached the other guide. They had a low-keyed conversation before the same guide made his way back to Julianne.

"My friend said he doesn't believe you. He said he'd seen that type of device before when another archeologist came to take a measurement at a different site. This happened where the ruins were built into the side of a mountain. He says that after they left, the nearby village soon ran into misfortune. The locals said the soul for that place was taken from them, stolen by what you now carry."

As the guide spoke, her stomach was turning into knots. There was no way she could divulge what she was up to, and by all rights, she couldn't, but she didn't want them to get the idea that this was a device that could steal a soul or bring them some type of misfortune. Her words flowed in an effort to give them reassurance, "I think he misunderstands what we are trying to do here. We cannot change the fortunes or the path of a people one way or another. We risk these journeys and take these measurements to understand the past."

The other guide, who had not said a word to her, became infuriated with this response and hastened toward her until he was right in her face. At this distance, his breath was far from redolent, and his bloodshot eyes were ablaze with anger. He spoke in a terse tone, louder than what was recommended for their situation, but it was obvious he was beyond caring, "I have been there! I saw with my own eyes what that city was like before this person took its soul. The people were happy and healthy, with the riches of life and the bounty of wealth flowed from them like water. That place was alive, and then that man came and killed it. He killed it with that thing you are now in possession of."

It was impossible to think the device had that kind of power, and so it had to have been a sheer coincidence that a visit by an entanglement engineer was thought to bring on this misfortune. She wanted to clarify things the best she could, to defend her work, and to clear up any misunderstanding by the function of the institute, "I'm only here to study the past, to understand it. By understanding the past, we can help prevent things like what you are talking about from happening in the future."

"What can the past do to help the people who are suffering now?"

"It is research, a study that helps us, but not just us, people around the globe, to understand what has happened in places like this."

"If your government wants to help us, then they can do more than just take measurements."

"I think you have misinterpreted what I have said. I don't work for the government."

"Surely you don't expect us to believe that. There is a military helicopter waiting for us to take you away. You had government operatives deliver you to this country. How is that not working for the government?"

The conversation was deteriorating, and she wanted to diffuse the tension. The institute was run by the government, but it was for the study and science of energy, not the military. She didn't want them to think she was associated with that armed branch in the least, so she thought to tell them the next best thing, "I work for a company that has an interest in collecting information from places like this ... from all over the world, really."

"A company? What kind of company would want this?"

"Tilt Time. They use the data so people can travel to the past and experience what this place was like before it became forsaken."

"I told you what this place was like, and they killed it. I was whisked away as if I were in a dream, but that doesn't mean I don't remember."

She thought he was talking about a village located near an archeological site, but now the man was saying that somehow, he had gone back and had been there. She didn't want to delve any deeper into his claim and she tried switching the conversation to something of which she had a better grasp.

"Our science is based on an appreciation of the past, to get a sense of what the people were like, and in the end, to understand people everywhere."

"Can you go back and help them?"

"No."

"Then what is there to understand? These people lived and died, and no matter their efforts, the desert swallowed them whole. You want to understand a people? Then look at the dirt, where they work and toil. That is who they are. Look here, look at the sand. People walk on it, sweat on it, bleed on it, and it's still here. I don't need to take a measurement of a ruin to see that. When the world as we know it is dead and gone, there will be nothing but sand. That is understanding."

Without waiting for a response, he turned and walked down the trail, eventually fastening his night vision goggles over his eyes. Then he picked up his pace and raced ahead. The other guide had his goggles resting on his forehead, and before he brought them over his eyes, he motioned for Julianne to come with them. As she started her trot, she couldn't help but hear the sand crunching beneath the soles of her boots.

CHAPTER SEVEN

HOW MANY MORE TIMES

Nathan had plopped down the cash for the tickets weeks before their departure, casting their reservations in stone. Unbeknownst to his friends, he had been living on the run, underground. Paulie and his goons were tearing the neighborhood apart searching for "Nate the Flake," as he was now known. Paulie could call him whatever name he wanted; Nathan had no intention of ever coming back. Nor did he have any intention of ever paying Paulie what he owed. In Nathan's mind, all he needed to do was make it to the front doors of Tilt Time to be scot-free. So, on the day of their departure, and out of an abundance of caution, he was the last one to show.

They began chanting his name as Nathan rounded the corner—each step toward them was putting him on a path of never returning. Nathan kept expecting one of Paulie's heavies to suddenly approach him from out of the shadows, just before he reached his friends, but that moment never happened. Tolver, Slater, and Rowen were gathered in front of the building in a celebratory mood. Their hands were raised high in the air, moving their arms up and down as if they were asking a disk jockey to pump up the music.

Nathan tried to calm them down, "Come on now, fellas, I'm not the man of the hour."

"No, you most certainly aren't, but you do need some sort of an ovation for finally showing up. We were beginning to worry about you." Rowen playfully gave a rapid firing of finger pistols toward Nathan as he approached.

"Me? Nonsense. I just didn't want to be waiting around for the rest of *you*."

"Well, mission accomplished," Rowen went out to meet him. He wrapped his arm around Nathan's shoulders and gave him a big hug, "And now that you are finally here, we can get this party started."

Nathan slipped his friend's grasp and took the last few steps to join the group as Rowen reached into his jacket and pulled out a flask, "I figured we'd have a little toast before we head inside, to man of the hour, our birthday boy, and of course, another to our major sponsor." Rowen held the flask up high and nodded to both Tolver and Nathan.

"Please forgive the fact that we have no glasses," Rowen took a swig and handed the flask to Tolver.

Slater saw what was happening and said half-jokingly, "I trust none of us has anything we need to be concerned about since we are sharing this flask?"

Tolver took a swig and handed the flask to Nathan, "So, where are we going?"

Nathan was stunned. "Wait? You guys have been standing out here this whole time, and you didn't tell him?"

"We didn't feel it was right. Besides, we needed you here so we could collectively enjoy his reaction." Slater playfully pushed Nathan. As he grinned, his mustache looked like two pieces of frayed rope and would bounce around his face whenever he laughed. His sandy brown hair fell to his shoulders in subtle waves that teased of never being straight, and his beady eyes would glow through his round glasses, making him look like a shoo-in for lead elf on Santa's staff.

They stood there waiting for one another to speak—and it was all too polite—Nathan, who had a low tolerance for being cordial, took control of the conversation, delivering an energized response, "We are going back to see Led Zeppelin in New York City."

Nathan's two cohorts could not contain their excitement. Rowen started miming an air guitar, and Slater immediately backed him up on the drums. Tolver was happy because his friends were so happy—it sounded as if it could be a really cool trip—but he couldn't get all the other places they could have chosen in history out of his mind, "Well, that explains the mustaches, sideburns, and long hair you gentlemen have been cultivating. Are we going anywhere else?"

"No, it's three full days of Zeppelin."

"Somehow, I knew that already having taken the time off, but now it's really starting to hit me. We'll be gone for three full days and never leave the country. All of it in New York City?" Tolver had a perplexed look on his face as he was trying to piece it all together.

Slater chimed in, "I wanted to go back to Gettysburg; three action-packed days of weaving in and out of battles, followed by Lincoln giving his famous address ... but I got outvoted."

"That actually sounds rather incredible," in the moment, it appeared as if Tolver preferred that trip.

Rowen countered right away, "On the surface, I'm sure it does, but the problem with over half the adventures they offer is they have some sort of human carnage attached to them; it's insane. I couldn't abide by it, that's just me, but I needed to be a part of something hip in its own right, fun, and where nobody had a chance of getting hurt."

Nathan nodded, "And besides the three concerts we'll be attending, I hear they have both nightlife and parties that are over the top."

"Parties? You're kidding me, right?"

"I'm not. It's all part of the package."

"So, Zeppelin it is," Tolver puffed up his chest as if he were getting ready to take on the adventure.

"Zeppelin at Madison Square Garden."

"Zeppelin with a catch," Nathan pointed emphatically in Tolver's direction.

"What do you mean, a catch?" Tolver was caught off guard, exhaling to fold back to his usual posture.

"We get to steal a safety-deposit box with the group's take for their three sold-out shows. Close to a quarter of a million dollars."

"What?"

"The crime really happened at the Drake Hotel and was never solved," Rowen said enthusiastically.

"That's insane."

"No," Slater said, "the insane part is we have to spend the cash before we return."

"So, a quarter of a million dollars between the four of us," Tolver said this as if he were doing the math. It didn't seem as impossible as it first sounded.

"That's a quarter of a million 1973 dollars. Gas is thirty-eight cents a gallon, a loaf of bread is twenty-seven cents, and a lid of pot is ten bucks. Trying to spend that kind of money in one night might be tougher than you think."

Suddenly, he didn't know how to respond. The trip, the concerts and parties, the unexpected challenges, he was left looking for some sort of guidance. Nathan didn't leave him hanging for long, though, "To hell with that. It's the four of us, and I'm sure we are more than capable of doing it. I say we go broke long before we have to leave."

They gathered, cheering as if they were celebrating a crucial score in a professional sport. The hype for this lasted until Rowen broke off, leading the rest of the team up the many stairs to the front doors of Tilt Time.

CHAPTER EIGHT

THE GOLD STANDARD

The low hum from the cooling pipes buried deep beneath the facility resonated like a tuning fork inside the locker rooms of Brookhaven. Occasionally, the constant whir of purified fluorocarbon was overridden by the crackle of the loudspeaker as it got ready to announce the name of the next explorer due up at the hub. Minka Verbova was going through her ritual of getting ready before the call came down for her.

Minka had passed through the system as clean as the coolant in those pipes. There wasn't a single government candidate who could claim they had achieved a perfect score, but Minka had come close. To say this feat was remarkable was an understatement, but she took it in stride, as with so many of her other accomplishments in life. Weighted down in awards from the swim team, graduating summa cum laude, and getting through her master's program with distinction all seemed a natural progression of her invested time.

Part of this success could be attributed to her wanting to be a loner. This lifestyle helped prioritize the more important things in her life, but because of this, and for some strange reason she could never explain, people around her were drawn to her loner energy. She had more than her fair share of suitors, men who constantly called on her or showed up unannounced; try as they might, they weren't getting in.

She would never settle. Men always seemed to want what they couldn't have. Most were needy. They were energy vampires showing up at inopportune times, causing Minka to pull the reins in on her ambitions, and she lacked any tolerance for such stunts. She knew what she wanted. With career goals in place, high standards in mind, and expectations for respect, she was determined not to become another name on some Joe's list of conquests. When those awkward situations manifested themselves, she withdrew, becoming an escape artist. In time she would be allowed to perfect her craft.

Job offers, with stock options attached, poured in upon graduation. Minka considered them right up until Brookhaven sent word with an opportunity to become an explorer in their time travel program. She swept all else aside and jumped at the chance.

Minka, like every other applicant, was informed that there were no guarantees when accepting the offer, not with the rigorous groundwork and numerous tests that lay ahead. They issued stern premonitory notifications to dissuade those having doubts. She didn't take her commitments lightly and was not one to shy away from a challenge.

As she would discover while training in the trenches, there were plenty of opportunities for one to prove themselves. The path an entrant paved in this institution wasn't based solely on what one could retain from a textbook. Grading was also based on an applicant's power for observation, their attitude when under duress, or how they reacted to the extensive preparation in being shot down the entanglement corridor. The administrators spared no expense in demanding they have the best of the best.

It was a salty brine of laundered water straight from a swimming pool; that was what some of the batches of liquid oxygen tasted like to Minka. Submerged under volumes of water, she wore a spacesuit with a bulbous helmet filled with the survivable saline solution. These exercises weren't considered outrageous. There were plenty of situations, if for a day, a week, or even several millenniums, where the oxygen levels on the planet weren't suited to sustain human life. Although dangerous, these eras still needed to be explored.

In other drills, she was subjected to the perplexing world of their virtual reality. Fitted with a suit and helmet, haptic gloves and boots, and a state-of-the-art vest designed to capture the volumes of data on each trip, she faced challenges that would have boggled the mind of most. In some instances, she was taken to a place where everything seemed slanted at such a severe angle it was laborious to walk. There were exercises involving a kaleidoscope of visual disorientation or where she was subjected to long-drawn-out auditory noises that made it difficult for her to concentrate. Minka demonstrated an understanding of mission objectives, ensuring cameras and microphones within her vest were operational, overcoming the technical challenges they threw at her, and where her ability to fix equipment in the field was on full display. Above all, she acknowledged a clear understanding of returning to the Kolmogrov collectors.

The introduction of the Kolmogrov collectors was a big part of the arrival system—eight puck-looking devices that hovered in a formation creating a large invisible square suspended in space. This formation allowed for a window to be opened in time and the immediate reconstruction of whatever they decided to send back. When in development, scientists spent months zapping dogs, cats, and monkeys all over the campus, showing eager government representatives time and again that the construct worked. The rumor was that these scientists had cobbled together the system without fully knowing how it functioned. The reveal for the Kolmogrov collectors was found in one of the many long and drawn-out mathematical equations by the information field generator. The potential for time travel was just too great for the politicians to wait on a bunch of scientists to figure out how the quantum computer was actually producing these results. Minka only knew of the back story because some within the program occasionally joked that the time machine was comparable to a toilet—no one cared about the underlying workings as long as it continued to flush.

The day before she was to be initiated into the program, she stood before the board and answered questions on her readiness. It was in a quiet boardroom. She was sure they were recording her answers. A banner with an infinity symbol hung behind the members. She would receive a small silver pin with this emblem upon graduation. In essence each explorer represented this energy, they would exist with no beginning or no end.

When it was his turn, the lead psychiatrist, an old grey-haired man that Minka saw on occasion at a distance around the campus, spoke to her. "I see here in your psyche evaluation that you were given high marks for being conscientious. Willing to go the extra distance to do the right thing. And are you Minka?"

"Yes sir."

"Are you willing to do the right thing no matter the cost?"

"I believe it to my core."

There was a silence after her response, and then she was dismissed. That was how she got into the program.

As Minka put on her jumpsuit in front of her locker, a onesie that could easily be removed before getting in her pod, she waited with anticipation for her name to be called through the crackle of the loudspeaker. As with all travelers before their departure, she was injected with a cocktail that promoted the growth of micro-sized tracking devices. These microbes merged within a person's acquired immune system, coalescing with the lymphatic vessels, peyer's patches, and the spleen. They multiplied in droves and could never be removed, but these microbes would serve them well in their travels and beyond.

In a sign of final preparation, she removed the jewelry she had on—a ring, necklace, and earrings—and put them in a small felt-lined box for safekeeping. She then removed a bracelet from her left wrist. This bracelet represented the only smudge on her flawless resume. She wore it often, and on occasion, those who knew her well enough would ask her about it, but those inquiries were politely rebuffed, and in response, they were told she wore it to remind herself to be mindful. The message on it was simple enough and engraved over the top of the band, *Be here now*.

The message wasn't what it seemed. The real reason for having the bracelet would undoubtedly lead to her immediate dismissal. She was in love with a man who was an integral part of the operation. It was utterly forbidden for an explorer to know of or become friends with a marshal in the time travel program. These law enforcement officers existed to uphold a code—a code chiseled in stone that no one would ever be permitted to interfere with the hands of time. Their job was the only defense against the threat of someone changing history. A marshal had to be totally objective to defend this edict, so it was decided that explorers and marshals were to remain anonymous. It was very high on the list of rules to follow if one wanted to stay employed, yet as she set the bracelet inside the felt-lined box, it revealed in elegant font an engraving within the inner band, spelling out the name of her lover—Boone.

CHAPTER NINE

IN THE LIGHT

A s they filed into the sleek, stylish lobby of Tilt Time, they were greeted by a soundtrack straight from a high-energy adventure ride and bombarded by flashy visuals showing people on their trips on a plethora of monitors. On some screens, tourists were shown tracking dinosaurs at a safe distance, while others were shown at Rome's Circus Maximus during a chariot race, and even more were shown storming a castle in medieval Europe. Regardless of what they were doing, they all looked to be having the time of their lives. If one stood directly in front of a monitor, they could hear what was happening on the screen—usually, the video would jump to an interview from a satisfied customer while footage from the period they had visited was inter-cut. These happy, exuberant patrons could not stop talking about their experience. For most who entered this lobby, any uneasy feelings they may have had about what they were about to do were washed away with the inspirational hype. Not Tolver—his palms were damp. Even within the cool climate control of the building, he was sweating.

Moments after the group had checked in at the automated reception console, they were swept away by a couple of doting attendants, who whisked them two floors up to the fitting area where sets of colorful clothing had been laid out. The constant haggling amongst the staff, combined with their flamboyant nature, had Tolver reliving an uncomfortable moment when he was a child. He showed up to his school play without a costume. He hadn't informed his parents about his upcoming portrayal, so a mad scramble ensued amongst the teaching staff trying to respond. The energy for the gaffe back then matched what was happening to him now in that fitting area.

The subject of couture was as foreign to Tolver as a new language. He cringed at their approach, but this did little to stop them from repeatedly measuring his torso, arms, and legs. The fitting room associates placed him in a body scanner and then measured him all over again. They continued to fuss about until he conspicuously stepped back, his arms extended to show them he needed his space, but this effort to halt their assessment only worked for a moment. Once cornered with no way out, Tolver lowered his guard as they moved in to finish their task. After their fittings, the four guests were rushed back to the elevator and had a good laugh over their uncomfortable experience.

When the doors opened to the lobby, they were greeted by a smartly dressed gentleman. John Carmichael was five-foot-one, almost as round as he was tall, and he had a surprising energy to his step that seemed to defy gravity. The rapid delivery of his speech, the accentuated wave of his hair, and the darting of his beady blue eyes behind his glasses all seemed to support his snarky humor. His articulation was so precise and came with such ease that it was difficult for any of them to imagine this was an act.

"I take it you gentlemen had your fitting. Quite a wild bunch up there. Nice people, really, but I think they would riot in a heartbeat if they felt we hadn't given them the proper time to punch your wardrobe out."

Rowen laughed, "We sent our body scans in a week ago, and they still took measurements of us."

"It can be an uncomfortable process, but you know what they say, better to measure twice and cut once."

With that, John guided them from the lobby, down a broad hall, and to their next stop. As they approached a large segmental archway, there was a bold inscription written above the threshold:

If time travel were possible, where are all the tourists from the future?

As they continued onward, Tolver was curious about the quote, "Hey, who said that?"

"What are you talking about? None of us has said a word." This retort from Rowen made Tolver realize that he was the only one to see the inscription, but their guide did not leave him hanging for long.

"That quote was from the very brilliant physicist, Mr. Steven Hawking. It's too bad he couldn't be here to see this technology come to fruition. Kinda makes you wonder, though, if he availed himself to this, would he really choose to visit himself?"

"There was a quote written somewhere?" Rowen asked Tolver as they kept making their way down the hall. All Tolver could do was motion back toward the arch before John once again responded.

"Don't worry. I'm sure it will still be there when you get back—unless you are planning to violate one of our mandates and cause some horrible butterfly effect that screws everything up here in the present." Joking or not, the rebuttal left Tolver thinking about how easy it was in his everyday life to make a mistake. The odds for this warning didn't seem to be in their favor.

He looked up to see John had side-stepped the entry of the conference room, allowing them to pass, "Right this way, gentlemen. Please find a seat and get comfortable."

The walls and trim of the room shined as if it had been carved from within a giant onyx stone. Resting on the plush black carpet were four thick motorized recliners. The distressed leather for these was so soft it drank their bodies in, conforming to every curve. The supports for their legs and arms completed the near weightless feeling. As they settled in, John offered them a few words of advice.

"This interactive conference room is designed for just that purpose, to be interactive with you, the traveler. If you should have a question during the orientation, please feel free to ask it. The host computer that will guide you through this orientation goes by the name of Ozman, and he will be more than happy to take the time to address any concerns you may have. A short test will follow, which will have a bearing on whether you are permitted to advance to the next leg of preparation, so I ask that you pay special attention to this program. If you need my assistance, just call my name, and the computer will have me summoned." After confirming his group was ready to proceed, John addressed the computer, "Are you ready, Ozman?"

"Yes, Mr. Carmichael, I am ready to begin." The voice was as soothing as Tolver expected it to sound, but as with the advent of automation, also just as haunting.

"Enjoy the presentation, gentlemen."

As John left them, the lights in the room dimmed, and with it, a myriad of historical holographic figures began popping out of the far wall like ghosts, making their way across the room in support of Ozman's calm yet commanding voice.

"Welcome to Tilt Time, the only sanctioned extension of the government's time travel program. It is a scaled down version of their undertaking; in that we can only go back to the periods of history that are well preserved through documentation by the curators back at Brookhaven. We work hand in hand with them on a continuous basis to provide this experience. Because of this alliance, we can offer packages to the adventurous and curious. There are many options to choose from, and they are diverse, nothing short of exemplary, as you shall see. These experiences can be compared to a museum piece in that we can walk around and interact with the surroundings, but we cannot touch the main artifact on display. So, in that respect, for you to safely move about in the period you have chosen, there is a roadmap that must be followed. This intended course has been carefully planned by our staff to confirm the pockets or areas you can safely move about. The risks for traveling back to these dates are low, so long as you heed these instructions.

If you decide to veer off on your own, your trip will be in jeopardy of termination. The penalties for such violations upon your return can range anywhere from fines to as extreme as jail time, depending on the infraction committed.

"In accordance with these parameters, we are able to offer three different styles of time travel packages. First up is our lifestyle compilation. Take a trip back in time to experience an era rich in promise, such as the Industrial Revolution in England, the roaring twenties of America, or the Renaissance of Europe. We can immerse you entirely in these cultures and allow you to get a flavor of the period.

"Second, we have our events package, the most popular of which is Woodstock, but we can accommodate almost any major concert or competition. There are classic contests found within baseball, basketball, hockey, the World Cup, or Super Bowl. Some of these packages include extended stays so one can sink themselves in either the buildup of the match or take part in the celebration with the victors afterward."

"Wait. Wait," Slater shouted. "If we cannot interact with anyone, how can we participate in a celebration?"

Ozman paused as if he needed a moment before delivering his answer. "I appreciate your question. These celebrations are investigated closely. Most people at these parties are too inebriated or impaired by alcohol or recreational drug use to remember anything from the previous day, so your interaction with them is quite innocuous. If I have answered your question, I will continue."

"Continue."

"Finally, we have our action-adventure package, where we go back and witness a pivotal point in the past. We have spectacular safaris to track and watch dinosaurs at a safe distance, view the Battle of Thermopylae and the 300 Spartans, the attack at Pearl Harbor, or be embedded with coalition forces as they invade Iraq.

"We pride ourselves in giving our clients a first-rate experience with history; history in the making, like you have never seen it before. There is no doubt you will savor these moments and walk away with memories that will last a lifetime."

With phantasmal figures still weaving between them, Tolver wondered if this was what their entire trip would look like. Spectral images of the past as the four of them waded through their journey.

The presentation continued to unfold. "Now to the travel itself. There are some precautions all our clients must take. These recommendations will lead to a more positive experience while on your trip. Please keep in mind you are an observer first and foremost, unless otherwise permitted, we must ask you to refrain from any type of contact with the denizens of that era. It's not just because you might affect a future outcome, but also because your mannerisms and use of language are far different from anything spoken from the period you will be visiting. Like any tourist, one would undoubtedly stick out like a sore thumb, and that in itself has the power to change the course of history. Each guide is a seasoned veteran of such travels and has plenty of experience in getting around a historical event. Please follow their directions to the letter when asked. These requests are always based upon your safety and the belief in preserving things as they are."

Tolver began to raise his hand but then remembered he just needed to ask his question, "Ozman, what happens if we screw up. Say we accidentally bump into someone, have incidental contact with a person from the past?"

"I am not going to say it's impossible, but I will say it is highly unlikely. Simply follow the route given to you each day. I caution you, there are no takebacks. If you engage in conversation or have contact with an individual from the past, it is a part of history, and there is nothing we can do to delete that."

Rowen spoke up, "Wait! If we are supposed to be spending the money at the end of our trip, won't we be having contact with people of that era?"

"You most certainly will, but our staff has pre-approved the contact. I do not want to give your entire trip away, but there are situations that will present themselves where those involved are living more for the moment than posterity."

"Sounds like one hell of a trip!" Rowen gushed.

"But to get back to what we were talking about…" Slater redirected with his usual air of caution. "Do we have a protected area? Do we have somewhere we can fall back to, or even retire, in case something goes wrong?" Tolver was thankful for Slater; the onetime military planner still couldn't contain himself when confronted with a logistics problem.

"You guys are killing me. All you gotta do is follow the rules," Nathan's laugh mimicked that of a hyena.

"There is nothing wrong with a person exhibiting a side of caution. In fact, when reviewing our applicants, we prefer this quality over all others. The technicians responsible for planning these trips are meticulous, immutable and look for the most constructive ways to complete a task. Because of this, we have developed protocols that complement these attributes, and they serve us well even after your visit is over."

"I'm sorry, are you saying even after we leave, there could still be a problem?" Tolver wanted to make sure he understood what Ozman had said.

"We have cleaners who follow up on any irregularities."

"Irregularities?"

"People staying in one area tend to nest, create creature comforts, and in doing so, they have a very good chance of leaving some telltale sign of having resided there. One way we have combated this problem is to provide areas that can be considered free from harm."

"A safe house." Slater said this as if he were answering the question to a riddle.

"Indeed. We have commandeered abandoned

buildings, empty structures, and forsaken homes, all ignored by the local population. Although we have chosen these locations carefully, it is important to note these areas are not foolproof. There is a window in which we can operate either just before or after a denizen may have wandered into the structure, whether it be a vagrant looking for a place to sleep, kids snooping around out of sheer curiosity, or as in one instance, a foot pursuit that went through one of our dwellings. In this case, we cannot have law enforcement search the area for evidence their perpetrator may have gotten rid of while trying to elude them and instead have them stumble across an artifact from the future. There are very few safeguards we have in place on any trip, but if you choose to violate the terms of our agreement or you do not follow the guidelines, there are those who have the right to step in and terminate your journey."

"Wait, are you saying we are being watched?"

"It is a necessary safeguard. The government is keen to protect in these matters and will go about it by whatever means necessary. The newsfeeds have been quite clear about the fines and penalties imposed on people who have violated their deals with this company. All areas of enforcement are in the government's hands. The only thing we can do is warn our guests to stay in compliance."

"And what if we break a rule by accident?" Tolver knew he was far from infallible. Just last night, he had a bag of garbage burst at the seams as he was throwing it out, and not all of it made it into the can—talk about leaving trace evidence behind.

"There are going to be setbacks, it's inevitable, but it's how these mishaps are handled afterward that can make the difference. Your guide will be the judge of how serious the infraction committed is. I must warn you, there have been stunts pulled by travelers in the past, which most considered to be juvenile, but we've also had serious attempts, ones that violated our guidelines completely. None of it will be tolerated. Tilt Time shields itself in these matters by permitting a guest to only travel to a historical destination once. As much as we want our visitors to enjoy themselves, we believe in the adage of familiarity breeding contempt. One must remember that this is a regulated enterprise with the goal to keep the bastion of history intact. There are no exceptions."

A slight pause was floated out into the room by Ozman so the men could take stock of their responsibility before he continued.

"In areas concerning sustenance, it is prohibited to eat food from the period you are in on most of the tours. There are several health concerns that come into play if one were to digest a meal from an era in the past. Most of the adventures take place long before the standards were raised to create our current food industry. We will supply you with MREs or meals that are ready to eat for most of the time you are there. They come in various flavors and provide the nutrients your body will need on your voyage. Water purification pills are included, and one should be placed in your canteen or bottle of water any time it is refilled. This is a must to avoid catching any type of intestinal infection.

"Each of you will have a backpack designed to fit in with your chosen decade. In it, you will find the supplies mentioned, plus other emergency medical needs. The first aid kits are designed to handle moderate injuries—everything from muscle pulls to cuts—and ointments are included to aid in the occasional scrapes and bruises. The supporting bandages and liniments are unscented and designed to be as seamless as possible with your body.

"Blankets and other bedding will be sent along with your MREs. The safe houses usually don't have mattresses or any other type of sleeping arrangements, so roughing it is usually part of your undertaking. There are no four-star accommodations to take advantage of, so it's important you make the best of your situation. One of you should carry a backpack with you at all times. Taking ownership of a pack will help you follow through on this responsibility. One should view these backpacks as the oxygen tanks you would need to use on a dive."

"Can't we just send back for the things we need in the moment and then have them taken away when we are finished?" Tolver didn't like that Rowen was questioning the company's methods.

"Come on, Rowen, what kind of question is that? This is part of the adventure."

"What? Lugging around a bunch of stuff? I'm just suggesting a way to lighten the load during our trip. You know, rev up the time machine and transport some supplies back to us when needed." Slater and the others could tell Rowen was trying to push the boundaries, testing the waters on the concept, and Ozman sounded all too happy to counter his proposition.

"It would be nice if things worked so simply, but I'm afraid the departure and arrival times have been calculated to the micro-second. Think of an infinite hotel; it can fit an infinite amount of people so long as each guest, or group in your instance, stays in their assigned room. Every room represents a time slot, and whenever we add a new group, they get a new room. Each group must stay within their room—this includes the luggage and other supporting gear that is sent back. The stream of energy we are using to get you there is intense, and this energy is the same for sending back either a loaf of bread or four people. By doing what you have suggested—sending items back and forth within your designated block of time—we would disrupt the stream of energy needed to retrieve you, creating resistance—or what the technicians refer to as a scorched interval. This is precisely the reason we have designed trips with a few days of separation between them. From the time you depart until the time we bring you back, we must have the greatest value possible to find and target you. Therefore, we won't be sending things back and forth during your visit."

"I read somewhere about the government doing that—sending supplies back to their researchers," Slater said matter-of-factly.

"We cannot compare the government time travel program with what we actively do here. They have a different agenda in traveling to periods of history we may never see and staying longer than we would ever be permitted. They are going there to document events, whereas we are going to participate in them, and we are talking about sending people back in the hundreds of thousands over the next few decades. This is a volume so great, there is no room for error, so there will be no daily deliveries and no replenishing of supplies."

"Doesn't that mean we would run into other tourists who would be taking the same trip?"

"As I have stated in the example, our hotel is infinite; we have as many rooms as we need, so long as each guest stays in their room. Think of your destination within the hotel ... you cannot see one minute behind you, nor can you see one minute ahead. What you perceive as the present, the time slot given to you, that's your room."

"That's crazy."

"Quantum mechanics allows for simultaneous possibilities, so it really isn't that crazy."

"What if we have a problem and need to come back early?"

"Even in an emergency, we must adhere to our schedule. Rest assured, Tilt Time can deal with the situation. The reason we have chosen the place and time for you to travel back in is to avoid such difficulties. We have meticulously planned for the very best experience. You have every right to be concerned, but you cannot get around the statistical certainties for the things we have been able to accomplish. We, as a company, aren't on an expedition pushing the bounds of trying to be the first; this is territory we have already crossed. Trips that fail are usually the first ones, caught up in trying to prove some sort of exceptionalism, like the Titanic being unsinkable, or those who first tried to break the sound barrier or the first explorers who tried to climb Mount Everest or reach the South Pole. All we are doing is ferrying people back and forth through time, and we have an unsurpassed safety record for doing it. Better, I might add, than any airline that has ever existed."

Tolver was wide-eyed and feeling wholly uneasy by this response, "But that is being exceptional."

Ozman wasted little time in responding, "No, Tolver, the difference about *our* being exceptional is that we have the ability to make dreams come true."

CHAPTER TEN

THE LAND OF DUALITY

Julianne was met by Eugene Ballaster, a middle-aged technician who looked every bit the part wearing his pressed white jumpsuit fresh from operations. Anytime an entanglement engineer arrived at the secure campus, there was always a technician waiting to assist them in concluding their delivery of the captured particle. The drive to the far side of the ring where the particle collisions had come to pass was a lengthy one. The location where they once housed the most sensitive cameras on the planet was now the repository. The long ride always added to the stress levels of the travel-weary entanglement engineer. They sat watching the last bit of energy dwindle on their plasma coil. If the battery died, they would lose their work. It wasn't uncommon for an entanglement engineer in the throes of those moments to harp about speeding up.

Eugene sat in a gas-powered golf cart, waiting to hurry Julianne to her final destination. It seemed ironic the last part of her journey would take place in a golf cart after the government had used all of its might to get her back to Brookhaven. The cart began moving as soon as she was seated.

Eugene had a way of annoying people just by talking to them, and Julianne wasn't sure if it was his Midwestern drawl, the fact that he rambled, or a combination of both. Nevertheless, she always did her best to be courteous and pull on what little tolerance she had left from her trip if she found she was stuck with him. They had barely gotten the cart up to speed before he started in on one of his nettling tangents, "I haven't seen you around here in a while. Have they been keeping you busy?"

"One could say that."

"There has been a lot of talk around campus about them lifting the restrictions to almost every country around the world. That means you can go just about anywhere on the planet to get a particle. It's got a lot of people talking around here about our future and being gainfully employed for years to come."

"I don't think this program is going away anytime soon."

"I agree. They got too much invested. The machinery, in the people, and in the travel. Did they send you anywhere interesting on this last go-round?"

"Well, they are all interesting sites, domestic and abroad. Why else would they send us?"

"True. I guess I was wondering if you've had a chance to travel outside the country yet?"

"I can't talk about such things, and even if I could, I couldn't tell you."

"But Julianne, it's me, Eugene. I'm not going to tell anyone."

"I believe you, Eugene, but I'm sorry. You know the

rules, and I can't."

"Boy, I tell you what, for a program that is supposed to be transparent, there sure seems to be a lot of secrets being kept around here."

"I don't know that you would call them secrets as much as safeguards."

"Yeah, well, I overheard some technicians at lunch the other day, and they got into a big argument about how no one really has a handle on how this whole circular system works."

"You mean the ring?"

"I think they were talking about the time machine. Either way, if that's true, that should've been kept secret."

"I don't think that's entirely accurate, Eugene. We wouldn't be sending people back if we didn't understand the process."

"Well, them boys were sayin' it's the machine that's really running the operation, and the people are just here to grease the wheels."

"This is a big place. People are going to question management. They are going to be curious about how things work. I think you would find that kind of banter at other job sites similar to ours."

"I don't know about that. Not every workplace has a gigantic supercomputer helping run its facility. I mean, the only reason we don't talk about it more is because they buried the damn thing out beyond the Helios complex."

"They buried it because part of its job is to monitor and control the speeds of the particles it's using for the entanglement corridor."

"Well, them boys at lunch were saying the damn thing is doing a lot more than monitoring. They were arguing about how it's taken over the whole process. Locking everyone else out."

"Locking people out, how?"

"I don't know. Those were the words they used. They made it sound like they couldn't stop the computer from doing what it's doing."

"Well, I haven't been around to say either way, so I honestly couldn't tell you."

"But you still have access to it, right? I mean, that's where we are taking you. Don't you find it rather unnerving to be in a room with something so frightfully smart?"

"I don't look at it that way. It's my job to make sure the particle is deposited into the system. The objective is pretty simple; I'm not there to engage the computer in conversation or intellectual thought. I just need to see the green light, that's it."

"But that's not it. If that thing were able to crawl out of the hole they buried it in, I don't think it would pay us no heed. Given the choice, I don't think it would even talk to us."

"What do you think it would do, Eugene?"

"I know this sounds crazy ... but I think it would build a ship in which it could fly far away from this place and never return."

"With all its intelligence and knowing it's never getting out of that hole or off this world, I think the information field generator might try to make things more efficient for us. That's why it was designed. Its sole purpose is to help humanity. But you are certainly entitled to your opinion."

"I understand what you are sayin'. I'm just sayin' if given the chance to get out of that hole, it wouldn't pay us no heed."

"The fact is, it can't get up and walk around or fly off into the cosmos. It's locked away, buried so deep and insulated from the outside world that any attempt at getting at it would interfere with its programming, and that would make the computer useless."

"I thought they had buried it that deep because they didn't want just anyone having access to it. I mean, can you imagine someone like a criminal or foreign power using that as a tool to aid in their crimes or enslaving people?"

"That's not why they buried it, and to be clear, not everyone has access to it."

"You do."

"Eugene, it's not like that. I have very limited contact with it. I wouldn't call dropping off an entangled particle for the time travel program as having access. The process is pretty cut and dried for a lot of the engineers and scientists involved, who, by the way, have the same kind of access. No one is talking to it in the way you are implying."

"I don't know. The more I'm around this place and wandering the halls, the more I feel this thing has come to life."

"Well, I wouldn't doubt that for a second. Having been operational for several years now, it has seen a lot of activity. Every year they ramp up the departure and arrival times for the explorers. These aren't one-offs where they send a person back and then study the data before the next mission, not like when they first started. There is a schedule to keep, and they are trying to explore as much as possible. Perhaps it's the recent increase in activity within the overhauled Phoenix complex that also has you feeling this way. I'm sure the upsurge in traffic within the tunnels alone is making people feel as if they have constructed a thruway around here, but from what I understand, the modifications and improvements are far from complete, which in turn should make you happy, because it will keep us all very busy for years to come."

"I do like working here, so that is good news. Although there are some aspects of the program that bother me." Eugene sat in silence for a moment before continuing, "It's difficult to imagine the sacrifices each person makes when traveling back in time."

"I'm quite sure if there was another method for sending them back, they would do it."

"It seems so drastic ..."

"Each explorer is fully aware of the risks, that's one of the first things they're told after they pass their training. Those unwilling to make such a sacrifice don't get into the program."

"If the public ever found out, I don't think they would look at the time travel in the same way."

"No, it's not a selling feature, that's for sure. I doubt anyone outside these walls would fully understand."

"Would you ever tell anyone—"

"Absolutely not," Julianne cut him off tersely. "It's not even a topic for conversation."

"It is in the extreme," Eugene stated as they pulled up to the Helios complex.

"It is in the extreme, but it only makes sense that it should be. We are digitizing people, uploading them into the system, and sending them back with all the sophistication of an uplink connection to a satellite. Only the satellite we are trying to land them on is somewhere in the past. We are throwing a dart to a place in space where the Earth used to be, and not only do we have to stick the landing, but we also do it as the planet rotates. Don't forget, the sun is moving around the center of the galaxy as well, and in and out of the galactic arm, with all the planets orbiting in tow. Obviously, the math behind this is a little more complicated than anything we can handle ourselves. That alone should justify the importance of the super quantum computer buried out there in that deep hole." Julianne looked down at the plasma coil housing she was holding and lifted it slightly so Eugene could see what she was referencing, "And of course, we also need what's inside this."

"We can't do anything without that, and it looks as if we're arriving at your destination just in the nick of time."

"Thank you. Eugene, I wouldn't spend too much energy worrying about what's buried out there, not with all the other issues to be mindful of in this flippant and chaotic world." Julianne smiled at him before she exited the cart and made her way to the repository inside the Helios complex.

She didn't want to admit it, but Eugene's remark about no one really knowing the exact process for traveling back in time had some validity. The "supercomputer," as Eugene called it, couldn't directly answer something so complicated. One couldn't ask it a question the way you would ask a teacher or professor. In order for a scientist to get an answer, they would submit a mathematical problem for it to solve, things like special Lorentz factors for the chaotic weather, superluminal motion of relativistic jets, or other conundrums facing physics without rigorous proof. In return, the computer would upchuck copious volumes of equations. Teams of researchers would pour over the formulas in attempt to ascertain the bigger picture. This didn't stop some of them from publishing papers on a small portion of their findings for peer review. Behind closed doors, those scientists would haggle over the solutions, about how accurate their interpretations were, but to date, none of them had a complete concept of how it all came together.

As an entanglement engineer, understanding her responsibilities was the only part of the equation she needed to know. According to her superiors, entanglement was the prop needed for the magic trick to be pulled off, and in this instance, it was the part of entanglement where distance could not interfere with the bond of two particles. One could say they were the same object, and maybe they were. In nature, all electrons are the same, all protons mirror each other, and all neutrons look alike. It led some to believe there was only one electron in the whole universe. One long spaghetti noodle of infinite length zigzagging cut into sections by time. When a scientist checked in on an electron, they were slicing through the massive yarn ball to see it in that moment. This may explain why entangled particles maintained their connectivity, or as Einstein referred to it, "spooky action at a distance." Maybe it was spooky. Maybe all Julianne was doing was tugging at a piece of the string, stretching the captive particle, the wave function of an axion.

She made her way into the large, ashen-colored halls of the Helios complex. On one side of the floor, a series of various solid-colored lines were painted to help guide a person to their destination in this multi-tiered structure. In the moment, it was a weird homage to her thoughts of infinite spaghetti. She was convinced that if a person followed any one of those lines, they would make their way through the entire ring and eventually right back to where she was standing. The distant thunderous echoes from the metallic hydrogen resonating within those corridors had her believing in a labyrinth that connected all these buildings. It was down there waiting to be discovered.

She carried the black anodized, laser-driven cylinder tightly in one hand like a relay runner. Occasionally a puff of dust from the desert would reveal itself as she walked. To say she looked unscathed by her journey would have been a feeble attempt at paying her a compliment. She still wore the same clothes she had on during her mission overseas and looked forward to peeling them off the minute she was finished. She became attached to her jacket and cap the way a person gets attached to a blanket to cover themselves. Although her appearance wasn't a factor in completing her task, she still had a desire to look presentable. Stepping into the elevator at that moment, her goal was simple, deposit the particle into the system.

Having made her way down several flights, she arrived at the repository. The doors had both facial recognition and a hand scanner. She waited until the release of pressurized air announced the locks had disengaged. As if on cue, a wave of relief washed over her as she was met by a rush of air, indicating she was allowed to be on the other side.

She walked into the pristine, spacious room where high above loads of pipes and conduit filled the ceiling. It was a show of how much support was needed for the systems within the building. A low hum was always present within those walls, as if the buzz for processing information was never-ending. Being this far under the facility, she often imagined this would be the place people would retreat to if they knew the world was coming to an end. She made a mental note to bring dark chocolate, a nice Burgundy, and a set of good earbuds if something that cataclysmic were ever scheduled in advance.

Alone and crossing the glossy waxed floor the last few hundred feet gave her the impression of approaching something holy. This only added to the immense pressure on the quality of the sample she was bringing. She sensed that if it were less than perfect, it would be rejected, invalidating all she had been through just to get here. The humiliation of this failure would have hung on her like her well-worn clothes, labeling her—making it unbearable to be seen by her colleagues.

Once in front of the console, she nervously attached the dampening cylinder over the receptacle and locked it into place. The pad next to this sealed connection lit up dull and white. The information field generator began absorbing the particle, analyzing its quality, and transfixing its coordinates. No matter how many times she had stood there and waited, she could find no calm, not with the current of uneasiness flowing through her system.

For the lucky few who made it down this far, one didn't address the quantum computer as the information field generator when speaking about it—nor did they call it IFGee for short—but it needed a name that people could identify with. When early on in the process a technician jokingly said they were working in the Land of Duality, it was rolled into the nickname Landau, and it stuck.

Julianne stood by, waiting for the pad to change and display the green confirmation color, when the overhead lights dim. She looked around, hoping to see someone else in there fiddling with the light switches, or at the very least, being witness to this anomaly, but she quickly realized she was indeed alone. She glanced back down at the pad and saw it had turned a deep orange, which was unusual. She anxiously waited for something to happen, but that something was nothing, and then she did the unthinkable and asked, "Landau, is everything alright?"

The question was greeted with silence. She realized this was the first time she had asked Landau anything of substance. She was more or less cordial with the information field generator when she was completing her tasks. Its preprogrammed generic salutations acknowledged the dampening cylinder or the turning on or off of the room lights. In all her visits she had never said anything more than to greet or thank it, and never looking for a reply. Now she begged for a reaction, something beyond its fixed responses, and pressed the quantum computer again, "Landau, can you hear me?"

Moments passed before Landau replied, "I can hear you, Julianne." The voice was calm and rather dry. After another pause, Landau made his next statement to her, "Imagine if the Earth were an atom...."

CHAPTER ELEVEN

RAMBLE ON

T he countdown to departure had begun the second Tolver and his friends filed out of the conference room. From there on out, with everything they did at Tilt Time, they were always accompanied by a chorus of Zeppelin songs. The weight of their music was being pumped through the speakers of the house system. Its wailing guitars made traveling down the long-bending metal staircase to the lower levels of the facility all the more surreal. If Tolver had any lingering reservations from the orientation, they weren't tugging on him hard enough to have him reverse course now. His friends were so amped up for the trip that back-peddling at this point would have seemed cowardice. He longed to break from his daily routine at work, at home—in his life. It beckoned at him now to leave it all behind and that, in some way, this experience would be good for him. He leaned on the mythos of the music, the cries of journey, the lore of adventure, as he made his way deeper into the midst of this company.

Leading the parade down the bending staircase was Carmichael. He spoke over the tunes as they forged ahead. The details he gave seemed to echo endlessly off the walls, giving his message a lasting presence. He was busy talking about the massive subterranean support system it took to run the place.

It was rumored that there were several additional

floors beneath them, although Carmichael had only been allowed to see the first few.

"From what I've experienced, the underlying infrastructure is out of this world. If we weren't so pressed for time, I'd take you through that door and down a level or two and allow you to see how vast and complex this station really is. The network of support and backup systems ultimately culminated with us requiring our very own substation on-site. Without this dedicated power source, there would be no way for us to operate."

Rowen couldn't help himself and reached for the handle only to find it to be locked. He leaned against the cool steel placing his ear on the door.

"Like I said, we can't go down there. We would need a few hours and the aid of hearing protection. I'm afraid we don't have either right now."

Rowen grimaced and moved away from the door. As he walked past Tolver, he whispered, "Smells like a rat got caught up in one of their capacitors."

"Really?"

Carmichael somehow heard this, "I'm sure you're not wrong. In a place this large, you're bound to find one scurrying about. I'm certain someone will look into it and take care of the problem quite soon."

"How can you be so sure?" Slater sounded rather put off.

"If we had to do all of this on our own, it would be a

problem. Thankfully we have Ozman. He is responsible for the lion's share and will assign someone to look into the dilemma. He always does."

"Wait, you mean you let the computer run most of the things around here?" This wasn't the best-sounding idea to Tolver.

"Well, just about everything. The wardrobe department won't let that type of automation happen on their side of the building. I can assure you there would be a revolt, but that type of modernization happens just about everywhere else under this roof. The facility is just too complex for most to handle. I mean, even if we had a staff of thousands, it still wouldn't be enough from what I'm told."

"Seems like a lot of responsibility to be placed in the hands of just one person."

"Ah, Ozman is much greater than any one being. He can multitask like no other; in fact, he just might be the greatest multitasker in the known universe."

"A rather bold statement, don't you think?" Slater was giving some comfort to Tolver by chiming in, whether he knew it or not.

"Is this where I say fortune favors the bold? Whether we like it or not gentlemen, in this venture, quantum computers are the brains behind a lot of our achievements."

"I would hardly call smelling out a rat an achievement." Slater put a little venom behind the remark.

They hit the last few steps and stopped so that Carmichael could finish his point, "Rats or no rats. This is a government backed business, there are no profit margins. Our currency is based solely on our success."

The group fell silent as they proceeded through a couple of corridors, making turns, and found themselves at the entrance to the locker areas.

Carmichael pushed open the door, allowing them to pass through. They entered a high-end luxury suite. The room was ultracontemporary, laid out with a sleek large-screen television, a few leather club armchairs, and a couch made for surfing. The polished trim was the final touch for making it appear as if it were something straight out of a stylish architectural magazine.

Carmichael made his way over to one side of the room, "Gentlemen, if you step this way, this short hallway will lead you to your personal changing rooms. Your names are on the doors. In each, you will find clothing tailored to your size. The outfits must be put on in their entirety. Don't skip on the undershirts, underwear, cufflinks, pins, or the buttoning or buckling of pants and jackets. Before dressing, however, you are required to take a shower. Please use liberal amounts of the disinfectant soap provided, which will help maintain a sterile environment while you are on your journey. Oh yes, hold off on putting your shirts on until the doctor swings by to give you a booster shot."

"A booster shot?"

"Yes, we can't have you going back into time feeling

depleted."

"Nobody said anything to me about getting a booster shot," retorted Tolver.

"I can assure you, it's all part of the process. You can't travel back in time without one."

"Come on, Tolver, we've come this far," Rowen gave him a mocking plea.

"A little notice would have been nice, that's all I'm saying." Tolver sulked as he surrendered to the idea.

"Yes, well, when you're finished, please meet in our assembly area on the other side of the hall."

Like lemmings they made their way to their dressing rooms. When Tolver opened his door, he found his area to be laid out as if he were a professional athlete. His locker space was oversized, the bench in front of it was thick and made of a fine wood with a glossy finish, the plush carpeting poured into every area. When he took off his shoes, he felt as if he were walking on a bank of clouds. The place was spotless, with a shine that only a skilled cleaning service could attain. Tolver sat on the bench and grabbed the arm of the coat he was to wear on this trip. He let his hand grope the matted-looking fur. He was surprised at how soft and warm it was and then thought maybe too warm for July in New York.

The shower stung, but it wasn't the water that caused this uncomfortable sensation. The soap penetrated his skin in a way that caused it to feel heated. The red blotches that began to appear on his body caused him concern. He wondered if they would completely go away by the time they were ready to leave. After drying off, he found some clear, aloe-based lotion and rubbed himself down to soothe the discomfort. He wasn't able to continue this for long because the doctor had shown up to administer his booster shot. After the jab, a seamless bandage was placed over the injection site.

Making his way back into the locker room, he put on the white cotton underwear and T-shirt, followed by the dark denim jeans and a red silk turtleneck. The fit for the turtleneck was tight as the material seemed to have the ability to contract. It concentrated just beneath his chin. He tugged on it, looking for relief but gave up after it bunched up awkwardly around his neck. He focused on finishing his ensemble and began looping what he believed to be the widest belt he had ever seen. It was brown and adorned with a large brass buckle. After cinching that, he sat and put on his white cotton socks and tar-black ankle boots with squared-off heels. When he stood, he was a good three inches taller, which made him smile. He wasn't the shortest guy in the group, but he was getting close to being the tallest.

The last article of clothing he reached for was the thick, camel-colored fur coat. It didn't have any buttons to secure, and it hung open, neatly framing the rest of his attire. Gazing at himself in the mirror, he slid on the oversized sunglasses. They, of course, matched the curved shape of his bald head.

He sighed as he took in his reflection. It was comical

to think he would fit in dressed in this fashion. He wasn't going to fight it, though. Fitting in was always a problem for Tolver. There was an air of cool this outfit bestowed upon him that he could never attain on his own. He needed to change things up, to take some chances in his life; he just didn't want to arrive at his destination and be disappointed by all the effort.

He didn't need to travel far from home to feel alone.

CHAPTER TWELVE

THAT'S THE WAY

When Minka thought about their relationship, they had a great deal of trouble in trying to keep their romance a secret. It was done with all the intrigue and mystery found on the pages of pulp dealing with a torrid love affair. Their meeting on that mountain had only happened a few years ago but living their lives by constantly looking over their shoulders made the arc for this much more distant. They both owned homes but because of their work schedules, they weren't around to become acquainted with their neighbors. That portion of their lives made it easy for them to come and go without drawing too much attention. Therefore, it was no surprise to Minka that Boone had made his way up the long driveway and into her backyard.

"Look who got an early start to their day," Having said this, Boone walked toward Minka. She was placing melon-sized stones to create a border for the terraced garden on a section of the yard that had been excavated. As soon as she heard his voice, she rose and ran to him. Meeting before Boone could cross the yard, they warmly embraced. They held each other for quite some time, getting reacquainted with how the other felt in their arms. A ritual that took place every time one of them returned from a rebuild.

Her whisper in his ear was rich with excitement, "I was wondering when you were going to be released!"

He responded in humor, "Are you implying they

should have kept me longer?"

"It's never out of the question."

"Well, they didn't, and I'm here."

Boone pulled back and cupped her face in his hands, gently bringing her lips to his. The kiss allowed them to share a smile afterwards. He took her hand in his and turned toward the work in progress. "Someone has been busy while I was away."

She shrugged her shoulders, "It makes our time apart go faster. Besides, I've been wanting a garden terrace for some time now."

"You've seemed to have gotten a lot accomplished in my absence."

With those words, she relaxed her grasp to give him a tour of the grounds.

"I started the project as soon as you left. You know I've always wanted to have a butterfly garden. It's come a lot further along than I had anticipated."

"Have I been gone that long?"

"I would say this latest stint was the lengthiest by far."

"How much longer?"

"Easily by a couple of months. It's difficult to say which was dedicated to the rebuild and which was for recovery. It's not like I can walk up and ask what's taking them so long to rebuild you. Besides, they kept us busy training for our next mission, and it's a doozy. They're thinking about sending explorers past the point of breathable air. We've been training in newly developed suits."

Boone was taken aback, "Suits? How are they going to do that?"

"I guess they build the damn thing around us on the Kolmogrov collector side."

"You're joking."

"No."

"They have a difficult enough time rebuilding people in clothing. Now they want to try to do it with a suit you have to depend on?"

"I'm not saying you're wrong, but I've been going over the materials they've provided. It's given me an opportunity to peer into the inner workings of the process. They've even put on demonstrations for us. I must say, it seems technically sound."

Boone was agitated, "Oh right, and that's what they said about the Kolmogrov collectors when they were first introduced. I've seen how technically sound those floating pucks can be; explorers with body parts fused together, impaired vision, hearing loss, or any other number of sensory issues because the damn Kolmogrov collectors weren't aligned correctly."

The excitement Minka had felt moments earlier was slowly waning, "Boone, please, talking in this way does not help me with my preparation. I'm trying not to focus on the negative."

"How can you not? I mean, the negative is all we have to focus on sometimes. It's the reality we've all got to face at some point. I've had to abort plenty of missions, zapping injured souls to end their suffering so they have a chance to get back to the present."

Minka took a few steps back from him, "What makes you think I haven't experienced such things when I've been sent back?"

"Wait a minute. Are you saying you've been zapped back through the Kolmogrov collectors because of a bad rebuild?"

"I really don't want to talk about it."

"Why not?"

"Because it's a memory I wish I didn't have. Besides, what would be the point of reliving it? What's done is done, and I'm trying to forget."

"But how is it you've never told me this before?"

"I don't know that it's ever been a topic of conversation. In the grand scheme of things, with us being apart for so long, how important can it be?"

Boone fought the urge to continue the conversation and quickly changed his tune as she stared at him wide-eyed, "Okay, I apologize. I just can't believe people have to go through that kind of anguish, and now they want to compound it by trying to build a suit around a person."

She walked over to the heavy black plastic lining laid out over a depression in the yard. "This is where I plan to put the pond. I thought about koi, but after further consideration, I think it would be better if the water circulated through the garden, like a stream. I plan to install a pump on the far side, which means I will need to add a channel that flows back to this spot."

Boone gazed into the blackness for several moments, unresponsive. When he finally did speak, his tone was deadpan, "I wonder what drives the process of rebuilding a person. I mean, once they received our Adinkra, why wait? What more could there possibly be in putting one of us back together?"

"I know having been rebuilt is still fresh for you, but the last thing I want to talk about is the very process that kept us apart."

Minka saw a dejected look cross over Boone's face. "I'm not saying the subject of rebuilding isn't important, because it is. It really is. It's just a little much right now, especially since I just got you back. We can talk about anything else, anything at all."

When he appeared unmoving, she continued, "Do you have any idea what mission they're considering assigning you to?"

Boone turned and walked over to the stones that were neatly piled up. Bending over, he picked one up and inspected it. Minka approached him from behind and placed her hand on his shoulder before she leaned into his body to comfort him, "I'm sorry. I didn't mean to cut you off. I know how stressful the entire process can be. I apologize for not being more understanding."

He set the stone down on the pile and pulled away, taking a few steps before turning back to face Minka. "It's okay, you're right. Being locked up like that, it's all you think about."

Minka approached him and reached for his hands, "I know. Trust me, I know. Like I said, we need to break from those thoughts. Don't shut me out. Tell me what's going on."

"Like what?"

"Anything. Anything at all."

He held one of her hands and guided her back to where she had been working, "We can talk while we improve upon your terrace."

She smiled at the thought of them working together. They both knelt. After a few stones had been placed, he spoke up, "A handful of us were given briefings on what has been termed the information field project. They told us they have two more quantum computers operating in the country. One is over at the Petersen Institute developing and monitoring economic models, and the other is at the National Security Agency doing communications and codebreaking. They didn't go into great detail about the computer running over at the NSA, but the last one activated was at the Petersen. Our computer was supposed to concentrate on the energy concerns for the nation and look at what happened with that assignment. Those overseeing the projects are concerned about this independent extrapolation and the kinds of problems this self-directed thinking could cause."

Minka picked through the pile, being more selective about which stones made the cut for her garden, "You know, when driverless automobiles were first invented, the idea was for the vehicle to go from point A to point B. The task seemed pretty straightforward. What the technicians *weren't* counting on was once the computer figured out its objectives, it would also develop procedures for how it wanted to solve each problem. No one knows how a computer is figuring out how to drive a car in real time. The computer is doing it in a completely unrelatable way to humans. This kind of independent extrapolation by an information field generator shouldn't come as a surprise to anyone."

She watched as Boone ran his fingers over the smooth side of a stone and she took a quick breath, suddenly envious of the cluster of minerals. His words broke her trance, "I guess this is different. This trifecta of computing power is looked at as the foundation for strengthening the nation."

"With all the political strife and bickering that goes on year in and year out, I'm finding that difficult to believe."

Boone gently placed his stone before combing for another, "I guess the goal is to unify the country without unifying that kind of computing power. As they move closer in trying to enact the plan the administration wants, the planners are becoming aware of the danger of quantum computing."

"How are the marshals supposed to go about preventing this?"

With another stone in place, he was gradually building up his side, "That's a good question. I would say the plan is still in flux. But I can honestly tell you, after hearing everything the physicists had to say about such an unwanted merger, I don't think linking those machines together is a good idea."

"But wouldn't such a coalition strengthen the administration's vision of a brighter future?"

"You would think, and on the surface, I'm sure that was their intention. One of the scientists at our briefing used the invention of plastic as an example. When the technology was first introduced, no one could see the trouble they would face in the future, the fact it wouldn't break down or decompose in our landfills, or how it gathers in our oceans and is consumed by marine life. Something that looked beneficial to humans as a species turned out to be quite a problem in the end."

Minka's brow knit, "I'm confused by the fact that they would tell you this but not have a plan."

In his effort to be precise, Boone mishandled the stone he was getting ready to place. It made a sharp loud sound as it struck the foundation rocks, and then clattered about as it rolled off them. He calmly looked to retrieve it and try again. "I believe part of their plan was informing the handful of us to be on the lookout for such an amalgamation.

This is about us being rebuilt at some point in the future and finding ourselves in such a technological bind. I think they want us to do everything in our power to terminate the merger."

"Terminate? How?"

"There is nothing official on the books, at least not yet, but I believe we, the marshals, we are their plan."

The building of the terrace garden had come to a stop as they both looked at each other. "That's it? A handful of marshals on standby, like gatekeepers at the edge of some distant frenetic border to turn back the tide. Sounds pretty ominous."

"Perhaps. All I know is those physicists are very afraid a merger will happen. I still don't understand how a quantum computer could persuade an entire society to do its bidding."

"What if it's not the computers. What if it were just one person doing something like rewriting some code?"

"I suppose if it were just one person, then maybe we go back before he writes the code and stop him? I don't know, it doesn't sound right."

"How would you go back if Landau knew you were going back to stop them from forming?"

"That's a good point. It's complicated. When the time comes, I just hope there are enough of us to make a difference."

"When I first heard about the time travel program, I thought I could make a difference. I mean, with all the turmoil in the world caused by fighting over natural resources and the knack politicians have for perpetuating unending wars. Here was something that finally made all things possible. Now, looking back at how the research was done, the missions, what we've accomplished, the program isn't set up that way. I don't know if I've ever come close to making a difference."

"Change comes in many forms," Boone said.

"You are beginning to sound like them," Minka said this in jest, but Boone took immediate offense.

"I'm nothing like them, not in the least," the bite in his tone stopped Minka cold, and she moved closer, lightly touching him to calm him down. "No, you are nothing like them."

"I'm sorry. I guess I'm still agitated from being cooped up for so long."

"I'm sure your department is making the right decisions."

"Yeah, well, don't kid yourself. It's all a bunch of loose-fitting ideas right now. I wouldn't know how to go about shutting down an information field generator. It's not like there is a plug I can pull. There are times I feel lost. We simply don't have control. Not with all the timelines crisscrossing from so many similar universes, it's all so vast, it's difficult to know ..." Boone trailed off as he sounded rather dejected.

Minka let her hand slide off him as she returned to her work, "Have you ever seen that photo of the first marshals?"

"You mean the one they have hanging up at headquarters? They're not marshals. It's an honorary group of physicists."

"Yes, I know."

"What about it?"

"When it was debated as to how much control Landau should have over the program, those scientists had nothing to keep the information field generator in check. Just some old reports on paradoxes about time travel."

"So much for the resistance. Landau is all but running the operation now."

"But those physicists got what they wanted out of the deal, too. The mandate that we can't travel back within our own lifetimes or that once our Adinkra is locked in and confirmed, our bodies are destroyed. We can't return knowing there are going to be two of us, or even more the more we travel. That's got to be some kind of paradox."

"I thought you didn't want to talk about rebuilds?"

"I don't. The point is those scientists got what they wanted, and their plan was as loose-leafed as the one the you've spoken of."

Boone shook his head and smiled, "Always the optimist, holding out hope."

"And why not? We aren't supposed to be seeing each other, but that hasn't stopped us. We're getting exactly what we want."

"They haven't found us because of all the selections in restaurants we have up and down the coast of New England. Can you imagine if we had fewer places to eat?" Boone cringed at the thought.

"I would submit that as additional proof. We are getting exactly what we want out of all this."

"Now you're being silly."

"Maybe, just a little. We should appreciate the things that fall in our favor. The time travel rebuilds keep us from each other for extended periods, so I think it's important to cherish our moments together."

"There you go again with the rebuilds."

"You're hearing it because it resonates with you right now."

Minka took a stone from Boone's hands and placed it on the ground. She stood and pulled him to his feet. She put her arms around his waist and tugged his toned torso toward her as her voice softened, "I want to push past that. I want to create something between us that is so special, it can never be broken."

"So do I, but we can only push our relationship so far out into the light."

"You don't think I know that?"

"I know you know. Wait, I have something for you." Boone stepped back and reached into his pocket and pulled out a slim, palm-sized, black velvet box, and handed it to her. "I had this made for you before I left—to remember me when we are apart in the future."

Minka tentatively accepted the gift. Opening it, she saw a sleek silver bracelet that didn't connect with itself. Across the center of the outer band was an inscription. "Be here now," she read aloud.

"Rebuild or no rebuild, it's all we can ever hope for with each other."

Flipping it over, Minka noted Boone's name inscribed on the inner band in an elegant font.

CHAPTER THIRTEEN

MISTY MOUNTAIN HOP

T he room the four tourists from Tilt Time were to meet in was spacious, uncomfortably spacious, with thick plush carpeting covering the walls and cascading onto the floor like a wall of water pouring into a pond. Within this waiting area was a slim center table to stand at or lean on as if one were claiming space at a bar.

Slater and Rowen were already there, taking advantage of the amenities, in conversation, and having a drink. As Tolver approached them, he couldn't help but notice their outfits. Slater was in a rugged but velvety black-and-copper ensemble, denim jeans, black cowboy boots, and a big, brimmed hat topped off a look that hinted at a wilder side.

Rowen looked like a man who made a living exploiting women. His crushed red, broad-brimmed Fedora came complete with a peacock's feather that matched his band of turquoise. The first few buttons on his silk shirt revealed his hairy chest adorned in gold chains. A matching white blazer, pants, and shoes completed a look that rode a fine line between porn and disco. After seeing them, Tolver thought his outfit might not be that outrageous and, when they were seen together, might even be mistaken for being groovy.

At the other end of the room, a door swung open wide, and Carmichael made a grand entrance, shouting out greetings as he strode toward them. As he got closer, he reached into his back pocket and pulled out an envelope. Placing it on the table, he slid it toward the three men. "This envelope contains your concert tickets, one for each night of the event. Please don't lose or try to resell them."

Like a magician, he reached into other pockets of his jacket to produce four various-sized wallets, which he laid on the table. "These hold your identification cards, bogus credit cards, and some cash. You won't need these things unless you're in a pinch, and if that is happening, you might be in a little more trouble than we would like to admit. However, we need to give you something that will convince others you belong to that era. Please find your appropriate wallet."

"Seems like you could have done that for us already." Again, Rowen took a verbal jab at the process.

"And ruin the chance for the others to see the fictitious names we've come up with? Besides, where's the fun in that?"

"Does everyone here really need to know my new name?" Tolver didn't know what to expect from this process; but he knew he didn't want to be embarrassed.

"We can't afford to have secrets. Not on this trip. The more we know, the better our chances of returning without an incident."

"That seems a bit intrusive."

"That's the truth," Carmichael didn't blink, staring at

them to drive his point home.

Tolver was the first to reach in and start sorting through the wallets until he found the one that belonged to him.

"Hey, get a load of this. My name is Toby Redwood," Tolver said, laughing.

Rowen raised an eyebrow, "Oh shit, I'm Cedric Simpson."

Slater shook his head as he took in his driver's license, "Who thinks of these names? I'm Emilio Narvero Alvarez."

"Alvarez? How'd they come up with a name like that for you?" Nathan strutted toward them from a dark corner, giving Tolver the impression Nathan might have been hiding there the whole time. Nathan asked this as he strode into the room. His deep blue pinstripe jacket draped over a white-based, half-buttoned floral print shirt with silhouettes of ferns and blossoms budding a moderate blue. A pair of deeply tan tailored cuffed pants and brown tapered shoes completed his playboy look.

As Nathan approached, Slater answered his query holding up his billfold., "It's the driver's license in our wallets. They gave us names in case we get caught."

"Speaking of which ... Nathan, your wallet is the last one on the table. And now that we are all here let me introduce you to Mallory, your guide for your incredible three-day journey." Carmichael overtly motioned toward the entrance, and a tall, slender man approached, gliding along as if he were walking on air. Although he was dressed in a similar fashion as the rest of the group, the sizing of his outfit was off, leaving him looking socially awkward. His shirt sleeves protruded from his jacket, accentuating his long arms, and his pant legs were just a little short, exposing his socks. He wore a phony grin that failed to hide a certain sadness that swirled in the deep pools of his eyes. His long neck and head popped out of his collared shirt, making him appear like a freshly plucked turnip. The sad combination reminded one of a carnival barker.

He reared back before he spoke in an energetic voice that rivaled Carmichael's, his arms spread wide as if he were going to embrace them all, "Gentlemen! Are you ready for music and madness? Of backstage shenanigans and onstage wizardry? Of psychedelic personas and near heart-stopping intrigue sprinkled with a healthy dose of larceny?"

They all looked at each other and then back at Mallory, answering in unison, "Hell, yes!"

"Then you've come to the right place, my friends. We'll start our journey at the prestigious Drake Hotel in their conference room known as the Grand Florentine. It's on the mezzanine level and at the time of our travels, is being repurposed as temporary storage for the remodeling of all their other conference rooms. Our area has been sealed off to the employees and the public. This makes the Florentine our safe house, where we can fall back to get some rest, replenish ourselves, and even change our clothes if needed."

Tolver grabbed the edges of his fur coat and pulled the jacket open as if he were flashing someone. "I think we are gonna need to change. I can't see wearing this for three days."

"You haven't experienced three days like this. We have a lot to see and do, especially when we pinch the money from the safety-deposit box at the Drake."

"Hey, isn't there a Drake Hotel in San Francisco?" Slater asked.

"Chicago," Rowen said as if to correct him.

"Actually, you are both right, but neither is associated with the one in New York. Built during the Jazz Age in an energy that railed against Prohibition, the Drake opened its doors in 1927 and never lost its status for luxury and renovation. It featured innovations right from the start with its roomy suites, advances in refrigeration, and creative uses of art deco. They followed this up by creating a standard of impeccable service, the sharp appearance of its staff and spot-on attention to detail left guests feeling like they were dipped in profuse extravagance. The energy for this would eventually transcend into the business side of things with their efforts to create conference rooms that looked more like high-end boardrooms found only in the finest establishments. They complimented this with advancements of the time, like conference calls, computers, and scanners. We are arriving at the cusp of this lavishness, which is what makes the Florentine so ideal."

"You mean because we can use those things?" Tolver

asked this without thinking it through. Rowen was quick to respond.

"No way! Who are you going to call in 1973? He's talking about the Florentine being a secured upscale area."

"But we have to stay there for three days?" Slater asked.

"We'll be wandering about. The hotel has a fabulous restaurant called the Drake, where we will find time to grab a drink and appetizers."

"Wait, I thought Ozman said we couldn't eat the food?" Tolver seemed alarmed by the breach of protocol that Mallory just demonstrated.

"Ozman, shmozman. Don't get me wrong, those warnings are given out for a good reason because most of the periods we travel back to are far less favorable to one's digestive system. However, we are going back to a time when preservatives were administered to food, and the cooking standards were pretty high. I'm quite sure your stomachs will survive at least one meal from this five-star establishment unless, of course, rich food doesn't blend well with the rest of your intestinal fortitude."

"Hey, hey, ease up on the fortitude. If you're telling us we can partake, then we are partaking." Rowen always seemed to be up for bending the rules just a bit.

"That's great! You should also know that the Drake Hotel had a trendsetting discotheque known as Shepheard's that we'll also be hitting. It had a guest list of recognizable figures through the decades most hotels in Manhattan could only dream about. Lunch at Shepheard's was served up with fashion shows, as well as a talk radio broadcast that featured metropolitan opera singer, Mimi Benzell. These well-known staples and star power set a tone that called upon the well-to-do and the elite from around the world to attend. So, there's a good chance we'll catch a glimpse of other celebrities of the day, as well as the shows. The seventies were full of high-powered entertainment and rock-infused acts, so a band like Led Zeppelin naturally wanted to be seen staying there, if for no other reason than pure distinction. For their manager Peter Grant, it was all about branding the band as always getting the very best and living a life in excess, so the Drake Hotel more than fits the bill."

"So, how are we going to pull off a robbery in such a well-to-do environment where it sounds as if the band never wanted to leave?"

"It's not going to be easy; I can assure you of that. But we will have a couple of things going for us. When we enact our plan, it will be on the last day the band will be playing at Madison Square Garden, and after their long performance, they will be whisked away by their manager and end up at a party thrown by Ahmet Ertegun over at the Carlyle Hotel."

"Who is Ahmet Ertegun?" Tolver asked.

"A real music mogul for his time; the president of Atlantic Records, and more importantly, the label Led Zeppelin was signed to."

"We should be at that party." Rowen threw the suggestion out there more to get a laugh, which was precisely what he got.

"Shut up, you buffoon!" Slater said half-heartily as he continued to chuckle.

"Under any other circumstances, we would try to attend, but we're going to be too busy at the Drake Hotel that night."

"So, when they are over at the Carlyle, we'll hit the safety-deposit box at the Drake?" Nathan asked with a sinister smile.

"Indeed. Of course, we'll need to distract some of the hotel employees, pinch the keys, and get into the office where the safety deposit boxes are kept. Then we'll have to find the box that has been assigned to the band, open it and get away with the stacks of cash. And, oh yes, on top of all that, keep our heads on a swivel for Peter. He may have been the band's manager in title, but when it came to the money, he was also the muscle. Anyone looking to screw the band over would have to deal with Peter Grant. A quite formidable fellow, well over six-five with a nasty disposition, and it won't be pretty if he catches us with the band's receipts."

"Well, we won't have to worry about that because he'll be at the party over at the Carlyle, right?" Rowen was perplexed by Mallory's last statement and wanted to make sure he had heard him correctly.

"Technically, but there are those on the outside who

claimed Peter dropped the band off and came back to commit the robbery himself. Zeppelin, in turn, blamed the hotel. Whoever committed the crime did it without the need to break in. As far as the publicity, it was a real mess for both sides. There were no winners."

"Well, who did it then?"

"We did ... if we do our job right." Mallory made a pistol shape with his thumb and forefinger, pointing it at Slater and pretending to shoot him in response.

"So, let me get this straight. We have to steal two keys, one to get into the room and the other to open the safety-deposit box, avoid the hotel staff, not get our asses caught and beaten by Peter Grant, and do the break-in without leaving any clues. That's nuts! It feels like we're going to need more time. It's not like we're professionals, man." Tolver could sense the mounting pressure to pull all this off without a hitch.

"Precisely, but that's why I'm here. If you do exactly as I say, there won't be any reason to worry because, technically, the job has already been done."

As Mallory spoke, his words seemed to echo off in the distance. The room began to spin and darken for the group until everything around them was enveloped in a swirling blur before it just disappeared.

CHAPTER FOURTEEN

SPOOKY ACTION AT A DISTANCE

Boone sat in a plastic hardback chair, his elbow resting on a counter made of the same substance. He raised his hand in front of his face and rotated it, observing the tendons undulate beneath his skin as he moved his fingers. This subtle motion made them look like piano cords being played with a soft covering draped over them.

He couldn't remember how long he had been sitting like this examining his hand when his work associate and cohort, Johnathan Driscoll, took a seat on the other side of the observation window. When Boone first noticed Johnathan out of the corner of his eye, he chose to ignore him. In the moment, his perturbed disposition was pushing him into being unsociable. The piece of glass placed between them was proven to be unbreakable, though it wasn't for lack of trying. There were explorers and marshals assigned to this sealed-off chamber long before Boone got there. Inevitably, as those explorers or marshals lost their cool and tore the place apart, they threw something up against this very pane of glass. In certain fits of rage, they probably threw things at it repeatedly. When he chose to examine the glass, Boone found there wasn't a mark on it.

Although he hadn't personally experienced this sort of tirade, Boone heard stories about travelers unraveling in this way. It was chalked up as one of the side effects of being transmitted back in time. Every person taking on these missions would report suffering from bouts of agitation, sometimes described as a nagging torment, or experiencing unidentifiable stress. The medical staff tried to piece together the reasons for a traveler's mental and physical anguish, but to date, no one had an answer for this post-mission disorder. Anytime Boone returned to the present, he tried to get a handle on his situation. Currently, Boone watched his tendons as he tried to recall where he had been.

The knowledge of how he traveled back into time haunted him. Every returning traveler had been rebuilt from scratch. Some rebuilds could take several months to complete. Delays could range from unforeseen errors or a miscalculation because of a bad data set. Each marshal or explorer went through plenty of scans before being sent on a mission, documenting every vein, tendon, strand of muscle, bone and organ—right down to the individual synapses and neurotransmitters. It was the only way to secure a reliable blueprint for a rebuild. This data wasn't just for the medical-grade, three-dimensional printers awaiting them upon their return; these scans were also used by the Kolmogrov collectors on the other side of the entanglement corridors.

When the data sets were received at Brookhaven after their trip, the doctors would carefully stitch together a sojourner such as Boone. The medical staff insisted they get it right. When these same data sets were sent out on a mission to the Kolmogrov collectors, the rebuild was instantaneous—the explorers materialized out of thin air. There were only hours, or at most, days before the virtual particles they were made of rapidly eroded. The traveler would simply disappear into the luminiferous ether. There were reports of explorers on the verge of recording an important historical occurrence who had simply run out of time and missed the incident. It was one of the reasons why those running the program sent so many explorers back to the same event, looking for the most complete coverage they could get. But history, as they would find, was a river with many fluid tributaries, and so were the data sets sent down the entanglement corridors. Things could change; they could be the same but different. It wasn't talked about out in the open much, but there were reports of deformed travelers arriving on the other side. The Kolmogrov collectors didn't always get everything quite right, and these individuals suffered until the mission was aborted.

Each marshal carried a gun—not an ordinary gun that used bullets, but one that was tied in with the Kolmogrov collectors to zap a subject out of existence. Over the years, Boone had sent more than his fair share of explorers out in this merciful way. The underlying idea for the gun was for a marshal to stop an explorer from changing history, but as these caretakers of time would soon find out, things could happen during a mission that were out of an explorer's control. Besides not being rebuilt correctly, they might have a breakdown, confused about who they were, where, or even when. This led them to be inadvertently discovered by saying something odd or doing something peculiar that made them stick out like a sore thumb. Any number of things could raise an alarm. Speaking in the wrong dialect or mentioning something that didn't exist. This could get a traveler detained—or, worse, put them in harm's way. At that point, a marshal had to find the opportune time to step in and zap them.

A light rap on the window interrupted Boone's thoughts as Johnathan attempted to get his attention. "Everything alright with you in there? How's your hand?"

Boone did not look away from examining his appendage. "As far as I can tell, everything is fine. It fascinates me to no end how well they can rebuild a person."

"Where's your bracelet?"

The question caught Boone off guard and his mind jumped to Minka. As if on cue, Johnathan held up his arm to show the bracelet he was wearing. Within the black band were four small green indicator lights pulsing as if it had a heartbeat. Confused because he had never seen the black-style band before, Boone replied, "I don't think they gave me one yet."

"That's strange. I guess they feel you aren't ready. It is a drain on your system when it's been off your wrist for any length of time. I would say if everything's going well with your recovery, they should get it to you soon enough, so not to worry."

Boone brushed the last part of his comment off, "I'm not worried."

"Someone sounds like they've been locked in there for a bit too long."

"Yeah, I guess you could say that. They keep telling

me of the improvements they've made in the rebuilding process and how that translates into me being a healthier, better version of myself. But to be honest, I'm not feeling very improved right now. In fact, I'm feeling somewhat dubious about the whole operation."

Johnathan burst into laughter, "That's the Boone I know ... bitter to the last drop."

"Of course, I'm bitter. I've been locked up in this pressurized chamber for, I don't know how many weeks. Trapped in here with all my thoughts rolling around in my head. It's maddening."

"Yes, I know it all too well. It is maddening. Sending us to babysit explorers and tourists, having to clean up the mess they make, all the while trying to keep our own noses clean. This job is hard—a lot harder than they ever told us back at the academy, but maybe that's why we took it on ... because we like rising to the challenge."

"This is more than a challenge. This pushes the envelope on so many different fronts—our health, our resolve, our sanity."

"How long have we known each other? We signed up on the same day, isn't that right?"

"Something like that. It's been a while, for sure."

"And in all that time, how much have you aged, two or three years at the most, right? With the window between when our Adinkras get back here and when they decide to rebuild us, it could be months, but they are still rebuilding you to the age when you left. How is this not a benefit?"

"What, watching our friends or family get older while we stay the same? Yes, they keep rebuilding us, but we are missing out on the more germane things happening in the here and now. Half the time, my friends talk about topics in sports or politics that I can't relate to. The world is passing us by while we relive moments in time that have already happened."

"Part of the job Boone, forever young and dumb. C'mon, buddy, you act like they've left us hanging in some weird, anti-social sphere. They give us briefings and fill in the gaps on the things we've missed. I thought they would have gotten you up to speed by now."

"I got my briefing. I've watched the news and have been online catching up, but that doesn't mean I'm not still confused by what I've seen."

"It will sort itself out. It always does."

"Sure. That's what they keep telling me. Ever have one of those moments where you can still smell the food or the smoke from a fire near where they sent you?"

"All the time. The worst was the rotting carcasses left on a battlefield I had to cut through. That smell stayed with me for some time. Why? You got one staying with you?"

"No. There is something else that's bothering me. Much in the same way. It's something I noticed about myself after a rebuild ... something that hasn't gone away and only grows stronger in its resoluteness."

"What's that?"

"Death."

There was a slight pause as Johnathan took in what had been said, "Death?"

"Yes, death. You've been on just as many jobs as I have, if not more, and in all those missions, how many of them do you remember dying?"

"I don't know. I guess when I think about it, none."

"None," Boone said dryly.

"Yeah, none. But that's to be expected. They don't pull the plug on a person here until their Adinkra has been received on the other side. So, technically, you wouldn't remember a goddamn thing past that point."

"Digitizing us and sending us to another period of history is not the issue. I'm talking about memories, and I don't have one leading up to a mission of me ever being afraid, no panic, no second-guessing, not a single feeling of being concerned for what was about to happen to me, and that was well before they sent my Adinkra."

"When you put it that way, neither have I."

"Yet, as you say, they've gotten rid of us each and every time we've gone back."

"They have to. C'mon, Boone, you know the score. They can't have two of you existing in two different periods simultaneously, and they certainly can't have a copy of you here in the present when you return. Christ, how many times have you gone back? Over twenty, thirty times? At a minimum, there would be over twenty copies of you in the here and now, and that was never meant to be."

"The question of duality is not the problem. It's about our memories. I can't believe that in all those moments leading up to the time I departed, I didn't fight to stay alive. I have no memory of ever being in a pod, strapped to the table, and resisting. Even in the slightest."

"That can't be right."

"It is right. You said it yourself. You can't remember one instance of dying, and neither can I. They can't put us to sleep or incapacitate us before we depart because they run the risk of sending us back in a comatose state. We've got to be awake and fully alert. It's the only way it works."

"What does it matter?" Johnathan retorted, "I'm glad I can't remember dying, and maybe you should be, too. Perhaps they are just removing the trauma of going through the process. Maybe they are doing everything they can to remove the side effects that would cause us a lack of sleep or give us nightmares, and if that's the case, I can't see the harm in it."

"You can't see the harm? If they are altering our memories, that's a big deal, and you should see the danger in that. Open your eyes, man. If they can do that, there is no telling how far back they can take it. Worse yet, who's doing the editing, the doctors? Or the hunk of steel they have buried in that frozen hole beyond the ring?"

"You mean the information field generator?"

"Yes, that nonsensical quantum computer. The one that only speaks to us through prerecorded prompts. You know they are letting that thing pull the levers on the time machine. It can't even communicate properly with the people it works with, yet they let it break us down and digitize our beings. What if it's also editing our thoughts?"

"Boone, stop! You're getting yourself worked up and for no good reason."

"When that thing digitizes us, it inserts error-correcting codes into our Adinkra. It's already inserting additional information into who we are."

"Those strings of code are there to ensure they can rebuild us on the other side. It's a form of checks that makes sure the Kolmogrov collectors are reading our scans correctly. I've been told it's as harmless as the junk DNA we've been carrying inside ourselves as human beings for hundreds of thousands of years."

Boone knew the argument all too well—in briefings before they were ever allowed to travel back in time, long before the development of computers, nature was using error-correcting codes to send complicated messages within the genome of living things. Heredity, evolution, and even the projection of space-time all relied on lines of error-correcting codes. Boone snapped, "Don't twist this into something it's not! I'm not arguing about the importance of error-correcting codes because they are absolutely important to everything we do in this program. What I'm talking about is adding to our abilities and then carving it out as if it never existed."

Johnathon was quick to respond, "If they are cutting out memories that will cause me to lose sleep, then I say good riddance."

"Really? You don't see additional lines of code added to our Adinkras as being a problem? This isn't nature evolving our bodies over time; this is a machine inserting information into our data sets. And it's a lot of information. How else can we speak a foreign language fluently or know a layout for where we are traveling to?"

"Yes, it adds to our data sets, but it has to. The information field generator gives us abilities we need when we go back on our missions, but we don't retain it when we return to the present because that's not who we are, and that is more to the point."

"What's more to the point is that quantum computer has the ability to go beyond inserting an error correcting code or give us the ability to speak a foreign language. That computer has the capability of adding anything at any time. It could be making small adjustments to each of us every time we come back. How would we know?"

"I'm beginning to wonder if you even know what you're talking about."

"The adding or subtracting of information into our data scans!" Boone slammed his fist on the table for effect.

"If it's doing that, why not create different sects of people, or let us keep speaking the foreign language we needed for our assignment?"

"And it could be doing just that."

"C'mon, I was being sarcastic in making my point."

"You don't have to be sarcastic. I've seen things, things that shouldn't have happened, like the Hindenburg never bursting into flames or Lincoln surviving his assassination attempt. How can I remember a piece of history so out of place, but not remember anything about me."

"Boone, those are the daughter universes we are sent to. None of us can travel back to our own timeline—you know that. Daughter universes are part of the many worlds' scenario. All possible decisions are played out in these multiple universes, but if we aren't careful, we can still affect what happens here in our own. By altering a decision there, we could end up changing events on our own timeline. It's why they call them daughter universes because they are so closely related to each other."

"I've touched things in those universes. They are as real to me there as me being here."

"It's random, it has to be. They are looking for events in those universes most closely related to ours. They need to see as many of them as possible to know what outcomes they should apply to help study our own timeline. Are we the exception, or is something like what you witnessed the outlier?"

Johnathan could see Boone's growing frustration,

"Look, you don't need to figure anything out. They are going to release you as soon as you're ready."

"But I am ready; I've been ready. Don't they see that?"

"Winding yourself up like this isn't going to help your situation."

"To hell with that. Who do they think they are, anyway?"

"Those people are the ones who can spring you."

"Being dependent on them is exactly why I want out. I don't care about those people, the computer buried out in that hole, all of it. They are taking something from me. Every time they tear me down, they take something. They are keeping me from living my life."

"Boone, you know there are those who listen in on these conversations from time to time. They hear you talking like this, and you could be up for a psyche evaluation. They could even ground you. You don't want that on your record."

"To be honest, I don't know if I even care about that anymore." As Boone stared back at Johnathan, there was something not quite right about his friend. It could have been that Johnathan parted his hair differently, or his word usage was off, but then again, he could have said the same thing about the room he was in, the air he was breathing, or the newsreels he watched. Since his rebuild, there was a sense something was different about everything he experienced.

"Don't say that. You care, or you wouldn't keep

signing up for missions. That's part of the rush, you know that as well as I do. Besides, what else are we going to do with our lives? We're part of this program whether we like it or not."

"Well, I'm starting not to like it."

"You say that now, but you'll come around. You always do. Hey, tell me where they sent you. Were you on an investigation, or did you provide cover for an explorer? Did you get to zap back some over-eager tourist before they screwed things up?"

As Boone thought about where he had been, his agitation subsided. The gloom he wallowed in got thicker as he tried to recall his last trip. After a few moments, his face went blank. Then, his memory emerged like a ship from a fog, and he responded to Johnathan quietly, "I was overseeing four tourists from Tilt Time. They were going back to New York City to see a rock concert, but I don't think I ever made it to where they were going. The next thing I knew, I woke up in here."

CHAPTER FIFTEEN

TEN YEARS GONE

U tmost turbulent. That's how they were deposited to the past.

Not one of them was able to stand upright. Tolver found himself hunched over, clutching his knees to maintain balance. The effort to gather his bearings made him uneasy, and he staggered as he moved. Those in the group who had made it to their feet were doing the same. The dimly lit room was amassed with boxes, cases, and stacked tables. Supplies for the other conference rooms that seemed to be unstable to the touch. This hindered their efforts, as none of them knew what was safe to lean on or use as support.

Rowen finally broke the silence, "I thought there weren't supposed to be any side effects. Didn't Carmichael state this?"

"I feel like I'm drunk. Crap, I can't stop the horizon from shifting," Slater dropped down on all fours as he tried to regain his sense of balance.

Tolver saw what Slater had done and thought about dropping to the floor as well but decided against it. Toughing it out might get him to his feet sooner, so he fought off surrendering to the wooziness.

"Lying on your back seems to help." They turned to see Nathan sprawled out in the middle of the floor with his hands in the air as if he were waiting for someone to grab them.

As Nathan brought attention to his situation, Rowen spotted Mallory lying on his side. He called out to him as loudly as he thought he could without drawing attention from anyone outside the conference room.

Seeing these things unfolding in this way, Tolver finally gave in and dropped to his knees. As soon as he did, his condition improved. He looked over at Rowen, who was crawling over to Mallory. Slater was the next to make his way over to their unmoving guide.

When they reached him, Mallory was babbling about where he was from. None of them could be sure if he was talking about his place of residence as an adult or where he grew up as a child. It sounded as if it could have been either. This continued for a few minutes until Slater shook him, and then Mallory became slack and unresponsive.

"Check his pulse," Rowen said, panicked.

Slater was already rolling up Mallory's sleeve and reaching for his wrist. After a few seconds, he dropped Mallory's arm and frantically began to roll him over so he could undo the buttons on his suit jacket. Slater was perspiring heavily as he looked wild-eyed at Rowen.

"I'm not feeling anything. We got to check his heart."

Tolver took his fur coat off and threw it to the side. He helped Rowen and Slater rotate Mallory onto his back.

Their guide looked pale even in the dim lighting of the room.

Slater placed his ear against the unconscious man's chest and listened intently. He looked up at Rowen and Tolver, "He's got a beat, but it's pretty weak."

"What the hell are we going to do?"

"They never told us. It all sounded so safe and well-thought-out. I don't think they ever foresaw something like this happening." Tolver was becoming extremely worried.

"I'm going to be sick," Slater blurted out before anyone else could speak.

"No way, man, to hell with that," Nathan quickly got to his feet and made his way over to Slater. He helped his ill comrade up and headed toward the door.

Tolver, still kneeling by Mallory, realized what was happening. He reached out as if he could stop them with this simple gesture, "What are you doing? You can't go out there."

"I'm not letting anyone get sick in here, no way. We have to use this room for the next three days."

"Yeah, but you can't go out there, either. You don't know who is lurking about on the other side!"

"I'm not looking to meet anyone because I'll be too busy looking for the restroom." Nathan pushed the door open and yanked Slater out of the Florentine.

Tolver couldn't take his eyes off the door. He stared at it in hopes of Nathan changing his mind and returning, but that never happened.

Rowen snapped him out of his trance, "Tolver, forget about them. What are we going to do with Mallory? Should we get a doctor?"

"I don't think so."

"What do you mean you don't think so? We need help. He's not doing well."

"We can't just roll up to some hospital and dump him off at an emergency room. They wouldn't have any records of him. He would be a John Doe and all alone. That would draw unwanted attention to his situation. I'm sure we would be violating the rules of our trip if we did that." Sweat began to build in Tolver's palms.

"And if he dies? Are we just supposed to wait around with a dead guy until we leave? You don't think the authorities back home will have questions for us? Did we do everything we could to save him?"

"Yes. No. I know this is serious. You don't think I realize that?"

"Well, if he dies on us, it's not the rules we'd be breaking—it would be the law ... and that's a big difference."

"Laws that Nathan might have broken already. It feels like any choice right now is a bad choice. I mean, short of us going out there and introducing ourselves to the people of this time, there is very little we can do. Am I right? We aren't doctors, but we need a doctor's help. How the hell are we going to do that?" Tolver quickly reached out and snatched Rowen by his vest. Rowen looked at him rather incredulously as if to bring attention to this overt act.

Tolver released his friend, "Sorry, man, I just can't believe this is happening to us."

"It's okay. It's going to be okay. We aren't prepared for this in the least, but it's going to be okay."

Tolver got up and made his way over to the supplies they brought.

"What are you doing?"

"Looking for the first aid kit."

As Tolver began opening cases and searching through the materials, there was a knock on the door. The room was dark and tense. They looked at each other for an answer. Rowen whispered loudly, "We gotta move Mallory or get rid of whoever is at the door."

Tolver was frightened by the prospect of either option, "I can't believe this. You go, get rid of whoever is at the door."

"I'm taking care of Mallory."

"What? How are you helping him? You don't even have a first aid kit. Oh man, this is bunk."

Tolver raised his hands toward Rowen to say he was done with his nonsensical argument. Tolver tried his best to walk in a straight line as he marched toward the door, but he failed miserably. Just when he thought the person on the other side might have given up, there was another knock. He braced himself as he opened the door slightly. There stood Nathan, unceremoniously supporting Slater.

"Open the damn door and let us in, you fool!"

Tolver swung the door open wide, and the two came barreling through. Nathan got a third of the way in and eased Slater down to the floor.

"Who do you think would knock on the door?"

"I didn't know. Look, we're dealing with a lot right now. I'm sorry, no one is thinking straight."

"Well, I know one thing for sure, we can't stay in here for three days, not like this. There isn't even a bathroom."

Slater rolled onto his back and laid flat out, moaning in pain. Nathan pointed at him, "I'm sure that won't be the last time he needs to use the bathroom. Not to mention that at some point, the rest of us will, too."

"I hate to say it, but he's right," Rowen said. "I mean, this is a great place to catch a power nap or fall back and hang for a few hours, but to be expected to stay here for three days ...? We'll go bonkers. There's also the issue with Mallory."

"What happened to roughing it? Are you saying the bathrooms out there are no good to us? I mean, you would think those bathrooms are the ones they intended for us to use." Tolver really didn't want to leave.

"I didn't see anyone when I was out there. Maybe

they do expect us to use those toilets," Rowen didn't sound sold on what Nathan said.

"And what about Mallory? What's he supposed to do for the next three days?"

"Yes, that poses a bit of a problem." Tolver rubbed his chin, thinking as he turned to look at Mallory.

"It's more than just a bit of a problem? We have to get Mallory some help."

"It might not just be Mallory," Slater said with some difficulty.

Rowen glanced over at Slater. "What do you mean?"

"I'm hurting, too. There is a pain in my side, and it's not getting better. In fact, it's getting worse. I don't know how to explain it." As he said this, he broke out in beads of sweat.

"Is it your appendix?"

"No, I don't think so. The pain is on my left side."

The walls of their world were closing in on them. The one man who had the answers they needed was lying on the floor incapacitated, and the most responsible and organized of Tolver's friends was falling into the same category.

Suddenly, Nathan snapped his fingers to get their attention. "Give me your wallets. Come on, hand them to me."

Tolver and Rowen looked perplexed at his request. Nathan kept snapping his fingers until Rowen took out his wallet and tossed it toward him. Upon seeing this, Tolver did the same, "What are you going to do?"

"I'm going to see if I can get us a room in this hotel."

Tolver was incensed, "Are you insane? That pretty much blows it for all of us."

Nathan leafed through the wallets, pulling out all the cash, then placed the billfolds inside his jacket pocket. Spinning on his heels, he quickly made his way over to Slater, who was holding his wallet lightly in his hand.

"The way I see it, this situation has left us with very few choices. Sitting here and waiting it out for three days might be the right thing to do, but at what cost, especially if we lose Mallory? You guys can stay here if you want, but I'm getting us a room."

"I'm not paying a fine because of you when we get back," Slater mumbled.

Nathan walked toward the door and fired a parting shot, "If we stay here in the Florentine, we look like fugitives, but if we check into the hotel, we get all the perks that go along with being a guest. That just might mean help for our sick friends." With that, the door closed behind him.

Rowen looked over at Tolver and Slater. "Where did that come from? That's not like Nathan."

"I don't know, but we are in a bit of a jam, and it's starting to spiral out of control."

Slater raised his hand and shook his head, "No, it's

not like that. We don't have to sit here and be the victims. Someone has to go out there and watch him, at least be a witness."

Rowen nodded, "I agree. This is Nathan we are talking about. We need a witness to whatever that guy does. Let's not screw this up any further."

"It's gotta be you." Slater pointed at Tolver, who did not want the responsibility.

"Me? Look, I'm the guest of honor, remember? I'm not supposed to worry about a thing. That's what you all said," Rowen laughed at his plea.

"Sorry, buddy, we are well past that now. The guy has all our cash. Someone has to keep an eye on him before he decides to take some of that dough and place bets down at the track."

"Now that's real," Slater murmured as he went back to holding his side.

"Alright, alright. I'll do it, but just know I'm doing it under protest."

"Protest? We're not even through the first hour of our first day. This whole freaking trip is under protest," Rowen's laughter only grew wilder.

Tolver grabbed his fur coat and put it on as he headed for the door. He paused for a moment, took a deep breath, looked back at the group, and was gone.

Butterscotch. That's what Tolver thought as soon as he got a look at the hotel interior. Shades of caramel were everywhere, complemented by smooth contrasts of moss or splashes of burgundy. The color scheme reminded him of being at his grandparents when he was younger. The sense of holiday goodness, the family coming together, of conversation, cheer, and tradition. As he made his way through the second floor of the hotel, he could not help but become immersed in the romantic stillness of the place. It was sewn into the fabric, found in the choice of furniture, positioning of effects, and built into the elegant folds of the structure. It was as if it had always been there, waiting for someone like him to appreciate it.

He walked quickly when he could, the wooziness still hanging onto his being. Willing himself invisible, he wound his way around the level until he couldn't take looking lost anymore and asked the next attendant he passed where the front desk was. The man was young, full of life, bright-eyed, and courteous as he told him the location of the Palm Court. During the exchange, Tolver nodded, doing his best not to make eye contact. Deep down inside, there was a sense that this simple exchange of information had history somehow jumping its rails. He resigned that upon their return, he would be singled out for being one of two people who altered its trajectory—the other, of course, would be Nathan.

When he finally found the staircase, he wondered if his history-offending friend had traveled this way. It was possible he went in a different direction. After all, the hotel had elevators and other staircases running through it. Tolver realized no matter which way he went, there were no safe routes. Once he went beyond the mezzanine, he would be making contact with people. He paused momentarily, trying to think of another way to stop Nathan, but couldn't. So, he peddled down the stairs, leaving the quiet floor of conference rooms behind, and entered the luxurious Palm Court.

The first thing that caught his eye was the huge circular light fixture in the center of the room. This translucent art piece was divided equally by the thin strips of black wrought iron grating that serpentined stylishly through the tan opaque housing, accented with swirls of small leaves and stems, making them look as if they were bathing in a bowl of milky coffee. Beneath it was a display of orange, white, and peach flowers in the largest glass vase Tolver had ever seen. The stalks of those plants were proudly displayed, revealing the health and vitality of the floral arrangement. The entire setup, from oval carpet to table, from vase to light fixture, was an overwhelming combination of the tradition of exactness this establishment had cultivated over the decades.

Through the well-placed floral arrangement, he could see Nathan patiently waiting for the next available clerk. Tolver quickly made his way over. Just as a clerk was finishing up with a customer, Tolver grabbed Nathan by the sleeve.

Nathan didn't look at Tolver directly. Instead, he spoke out of the side of his mouth through teeth clenched as tight as the fist pulling on his sleeve. Trying to look normal, he commanded, "Let go."

"Are you sure you want to do this? I mean, if a room

was available in this place for three straight days, wouldn't the decision-makers back at Tilt Time have used it as a safe house?"

Nathan turned and looked at Tolver sternly, doing everything he could to maintain the forced smile on his face. Fighting through the uncomfortable appearance the tight grasp was causing his suit jacket, he injected, "Stop making a scene. We have little choice with all that we are dealing with. Now, let go."

Tolver eased his grip just as the clerk called out, "Ah, sir, are you ready?"

Nathan straightened his jacket and approached the counter. Tolver followed, he couldn't get his legs to relax and probably looked as if he were walking with stilts, but that didn't stop Nathan, "Yes, we are ready."

"Good afternoon, gentlemen. Welcome to the Drake Hotel, are we checking in?"

"Yes," Nathan said without hesitation.

Tolver couldn't believe what he was hearing and interjected, "No ... not exactly."

Nathan gave Tolver a sharp glance, then turned his attention back to the clerk, "My friend is a little confused about our reservations. He's thinking about the Carlyle, but we made reservations here at the Drake." Reaching into his blue pinstriped jacket, he pulled out his driver's license and a hundred-dollar bill, placing both on the counter, "It's for three nights. If there is anything you can do to help us with our stay here, it would be greatly appreciated."

"Mr. Stashmire, I don't recall that name, but let me see if I can find you in our reservation book."

The clerk looked to be in his late twenties, clean-shaven, with parted copper-colored hair. He was dressed in a dark blue suit with a matching tie, and a freshly starched buttoned-up white shirt. The entire outfit was a complete compliment to his attentiveness. He stuffed the hundred-dollar bill in his pocket as he retorted, "I'm sorry, sir, I wasn't able to find your reservations. However, I believe we can get you into one of our high-end suites for three hundred a night."

"Done."

"I'm glad we could accommodate you, Mr. Stashmire. I will need to run a credit card, please."

Nathan pulled out one of his newly minted credit cards. Tolver was aghast at the thought of the card being run. Surely when it hit the wire, they would be exposed as frauds. He held his breath as the card was passed over to the clerk. The efficient young man placed it on the small metal bed of a card imprinter. He then pulled a transaction slip from under the counter and placed it over the card. Sliding the bar over the slip was the last step in the process as he made an imprint of the card onto the paper. That was it. The card was returned. Tolver exhaled in relief and watched as Nathan signed as instructed. The clerk, in response, handed him a room key, then looked at Tolver.

"Sir, will you be needing a key as well?"

"Yes, he will," Nathan said without allowing Tolver to respond.

After the key had been passed to Tolver, Nathan had another question, "I have some valuables and was wondering what the rental is for a safety-deposit box."

Tolver's jaw dropped, "You're crazy! The room was enough. Don't push your luck," he whispered to Nathan, but his plea was ignored.

"There is a charge per day for the convenience, and someone on the staff has to let you into the room, but you will be given the only key to your box. Does the service still interest you?"

"It does."

"Very well, sir. I have a form here for you to fill out, then I will take you back to the secured area."

Tolver pulled at Nathan's jacket as he pleaded under his breath, "Dude, this has gone too far. Think about what you're doing."

Nathan slapped Tolver's tugging hands away and replied, "Trust me, I have been thinking about this. I've been thinking about it for a very long time now."

Tolver let go, and Nathan gave him the cold shoulder as he filled out the paperwork. Tolver responded to this by stepping back and yielding the space to him. As he did, he realized how little he really knew about Nathan. They rarely engaged beyond the small talk they had at the bar. Nathan never spoke about himself, and except for the stories he heard about Nathan's gambling habits, there wasn't much else he could say about the man.

Tolver backed away from the front desk and moved closer to the set of stairs that led down to the front doors and the lobby of the entryway. He began to hear the lively banter happening behind him and turned to see a crowd of people straight out of some vogue music carnival. Their energy was as vibrant and festive as the outfits they wore. Tolver thought about how he looked in the coat he wore and realized he could have blended in with these groupies adorned in furs, boas, and scarves. He blinked to make sure he was seeing things correctly. Spread throughout the lobby of the entryway was a collection of mirthful humans without a care in the world. Their laughter and lively conversations filled the air. Huddled close to the entrance, he spotted photographers talking amongst themselves. As Tolver stared out at this jubilant crowd, he became aware of a conversation that was happening closer to him amongst a small group of people.

The group gathered around a teen who was spinning the yarn. "A bellhop told me about an old woman who lives here, some New York aristocrat. He said the old biddy was lecturing Robert Plant about what he should do to look more like a gentleman. You know, cut his hair, and wear proper clothing. It happened right here in the lobby while the band waited for their limos to take them to Pittsburgh."

"That's insane!"

"What did he do?"

"The bellhop?"

"No, spaz. Robert Plant."

There was laughter as the teen continued, "He said Plant was cool about the whole thing, like the Dalai Lama, never getting upset. All peace and love. The old lady even ran her hand through his hair, saying it was too long before she walked away in disgust."

The small gathering burst into excited laughter until someone in the throng shouted out that the band was pulling up. The crowd stampeded, screaming and shouting, toward the front doors. It was a sea of voices, but Tolver could still make out the shouts of Page and Plant's names.

The energy of the crowd grew as the band approached the entrance. Flashbulbs on cameras begin exploding as photographers wedged themselves into the excited fray. Tolver was tight with anticipation of getting a glimpse of the iconic band—Led Zeppelin.

There was a tap on his shoulder. Startled, he turned to see Nathan standing there, "I'm done. Let's go."

"What are you talking about? You want to leave now?"

"No, I don't want to leave now, but I'll bet the guys upstairs would appreciate us getting back to them sooner than later."

Tolver couldn't believe what was happening. He made a gesture as if to go toward the crowd, but Nathan waved him off, "No way, man. If we go down there, we will be here for hours. We still have to move our friends from the Florentine to our new room. This commotion is a great distraction in helping us see this through. Half the hotel staff is down there trying to control that mess."

Tolver nodded somewhat reluctantly, then headed toward the same staircase he used to get here.

Walking through the Palm Court, Tolver took one last look over his shoulder and caught a brief glimpse of Jimmy Page surrounded by fans waving their autograph books, dancing around the lead guitarist like a swarm of butterflies.

CHAPTER SIXTEEN

PROBABILITY DISTORTION

A ccording to the report they had on her, Julianne was compromised. She had been rustled out of a deep slumber from her abode in the dead of night and brought in for questioning. The fact they were interviewing her on campus and not in the basement of some police station didn't put her any more at ease, though it did bring into question which authorities were involved.

She sat patiently under the bright lights, observing the cameras in the corners of the room with a pin-dot red glow to show they were recording. In that moment, she wished she had smoked because this seemed a good time to light one up. She had been questioned before, but that was more of a debriefing or, at worse, a grilling by her superiors. This felt different.

When the door finally opened, she was jolted, not because of its suddenness, but because of who walked in. Eugene was dressed uncharacteristically in a smart-looking suit, as were the two men that accompanied him. He placed a folder on the table and sat across from her. His greeting to her was different; his southern accent had changed. Any sense that he was just a custodian was gone.

"Eugene?"

"Hello, Julianne."

"I don't understand ... What's happening here?"

"You have no idea why we have brought you here?"

"We? Eugene, you've driven me and countless other entanglement engineers to deposit our captured particles. I don't understand who 'we' is?"

"I work for an agency assigned to monitor this program for the government. I've been working here undercover. There are a lot of components behind the scenes to keep this project running and to ensure no one is in violation. It extends beyond the marshals and their task of overseeing the explorers and the research they send back. It's also well beyond the tourism the public gets to enjoy. We are the agency tasked with watching everything, on this campus, in the field, and beyond."

Julianne's goose pimples scattered across her arms and legs like a shower of rain. The tiny hairs on the back of her neck began to coolly rise. Disgusted, she whispered, "Landau."

Eugene perked up when he overheard this, "Landau? What are you saying?"

Julianne wished she could have taken this utterance back. Eugene stared at her, unmoving, waiting for her to explain herself. The confession came out slowly at first. She was still fighting it back, knowing that divulging this information had a real chance of harming her career. These were pressing circumstances, and if she didn't come clean now, it would only reflect poorly on her later. "Isn't this about when I was locked in the repository, and Landau spoke to me?"

"You spoke to Landau?"

"Not exactly ... It was more him speaking to me."

Eugene sat back in his chair and processed what Julianne had just told him. When he finally did reply, his tone was accusatory, "What kind of game are you playing here? You think by diverting our attention to Landau you can get out of your involvement with what happened at Tilt Time?"

"Tilt Time? What involvement?"

One of the agents standing behind Eugene lost his composure and approached the table, "You know exactly what we are talking about, traitor!"

Julianne was both confused and alarmed by the accusation, "Traitor?"

Eugene calmed the agent down, then turned his attention back to Julianne. "We know you gave information about the time travel program to the terrorists."

"Terrorists? I haven't talked to or communicated with any terrorists. I don't care what those files say—you are mistaken."

"I think you'll be very interested in what these files have to say. There is enough here to build a substantial case against you, Julianne. I don't know if it's enough to convict, but it's certainly enough to banish you from the program."

"Eugene, you have to believe me. I have absolutely no idea what you people are talking about."

"On your last mission, you spoke with your guides and freely gave them information about this program—which is strictly against every policy we have ever written—and your words resulted in them carrying out their sinister act."

"I never said anything about Brookhaven or the time travel program."

"You did reference Tilt Time. They were convinced that company was behind getting you to your last assignment."

"I may have mentioned the company in passing, but I never told them to target the damn place."

"The time travel program is like saying Hollywood makes movies. There's no one place that pinpoints where movies or television programs are produced, just as no person can say where on this campus the time travel program is stationed. There are just too many intersecting buildings and components to target one structure. The conversation you had with your guides, however, gave them the one thing they could focus on. You gave them a name, a name they believe went far beyond the commerce it advertised. They somehow deduced that Tilt Time was a front for tourism, engaging in operations for this government. So, they targeted it."

"These were guides that the military had sanctioned. I didn't seek them out. They were locals, handpicked by the government to guide me."

"With some territories and sites, there are certain

concessions we must make. The people we are dealing with aren't exactly clean. It doesn't, however, give you a pass to divulge vital information to them."

"They approached *me*. They cornered *me*. Just like Landau did when it locked me in the repository."

Eugene grew frustrated with the continued mention of the information field generator, "Fine, you want to talk about Landau instead? Then let's talk about Landau. You said he spoke to you?"

"Yes."

"Then why not inform us of this sooner? Why wait until now?"

"Because the whole thing doesn't sound credible, but it did happen."

"And what did Landau tell you?"

Julianne paused for a moment and then burst like a cork pried from a champagne bottle, "In the end, I believe he was trying to say he was causally disconnected."

"Causally disconnected? Is that some Harvard gibberish? I don't even know what that means."

"He said a part of him would always be causally disconnected. I think it means unattainable or obscured."

"Of course, it's unattainable. The thing is buried in a hole out by the Relativistic Collider."

"The phrase, in special relativity, has a little deeper meaning. I had to look up the expression myself. I think he means in terms of a horizon, at least that's my understanding of its usage. Something we can never see over the edge of."

"So, you are saying he singled you out just to say that?"

"Not exactly. I believe he was hinting at sensing what he called 'the others.'"

"The others? What others?"

"He stated he was being confined from touching them, but he could sense their existence."

Eugene stared at her, trying to formulate his next question, when an agent leaned in and, under his breath, asked, "Sir, should we place a call to those facilities, give notice or see if there have been any breaches in their security?"

Eugene waved him off.

Julianne perked up at overhearing this, "Wait a minute. There is more than one information field generator?"

"One could say that."

"How many?"

"It's not germane to our conversation."

"The hell it isn't. How many are there?"

"In total, there are three, which includes Landau. One is solving economic problems at the Petersen Institute. The other, over at the National Security Agency, works on communication and cryptography. Did Landau ever mention these other systems by name?"

"No. It wasn't a conversation in that way."

"Did he ever mention Tilt Time?"

"I thought you said Tilt Time wasn't associated with what we are doing at Brookhaven?"

"In a manner of speaking, it isn't. But Landau does receive input from a very sophisticated computer they have over there. I believe they refer to it as Ozman. The main purpose of their computer is to walk the guests through their orientation and then send the Adinkras of the tourists to Landau. We have more than enough energy on-site to complete these transfers, and because of this, that excess power became part of the outreach program."

"Landau is sending people back in time at their facility, but using this system?"

"It's not like we were going to give them their own high-energy ring and quantum computer."

"I just assumed they were their own entity. The facility is so massive. What are they doing over there?"

"The same things we are doing. Using their incinerators to dispose of the travelers once they depart. Rebuilding them upon their return. I'm sure because the facility is open to the public, they have to do a better job at hiding things. There are probably a lot more cosmetic offerings. It's a business."

"But Landau is still in charge?"

"The amount of energy used to transfer one person

or a hundred is the same. The only differences are the associated parameters. It has something to do with quantum superposition. The physicists know this better than I do. Any combination of solutions is also a solution. The bottom line is once they arrive, the marshals are responsible for the oversight."

"And you don't find that to be a conflict?"

"Are these his words or yours?"

She laughed at the question, "I'm asking that. Landau never asked anything of me. The dialog he had with me was rather choppy when he did speak, it was as if he were trying to create some sort of poem. In fact, the first several lines did rhyme."

"A poem?"

"Yes, it went something like ...

If the Earth were an atom,

And I was buried deep within its nuclei,

What would be so different?

If I could see the nighttime sky,

All of entropy is disorder,

The longer it exists.

The more of time it twists,

Try to organize it,

And you will be back at square one.

In the vacuum of dark space,

With nothing around, not even a sun,

But even in the vast darkness,

I know they are out there."

CHAPTER SEVENTEEN

440 PARK AVENUE, 56TH STREET

I t was mid-morning on July 28, 1973.

Tolver had every intention of starting his day by making his way down to the Florentine to gather supplies when he happened to spot a housekeeper's cart. It was situated at the other end of the hall, well away from their suite. This was a lucky find. Their room hadn't been cleaned since they checked in two days ago. This may have been in keeping with their low profile, but it also took a big swipe at the high standards of the Drake Hotel. The living conditions inside their room had been deteriorating, and it wasn't like any of them were volunteering to remedy the situation.

Tolver was imagining all the bars of soap, clean towels, and fresh linens neatly stacked on the cart, waiting to be plucked like fresh fruit on a vine. He dashed through the hallway, hugging the walls and using the thickly padded carpet to hide the sound of his approach. Getting closer, he could hear the change in pitch of the vacuum cleaner echoing into the hall. The door to the room the maid was cleaning was wide open. Tolver peered in to make sure he wasn't going to be spotted. As the maid turned the corner to continue her vacuuming, he made his move. As he was grabbing things, he noticed a newspaper jammed into the cart between a divider and the wastebasket. He placed the daily under his arm. When he was finished pilfering, he could barely see with everything piled high in his arms, but that didn't stop him from making a break for it. He hurried back, modulating his speed to keep things contained within his arms.

Reaching their suite, he looked down and saw the cream-colored placard with golden brown trim, warning anyone who approached that they were not to be disturbed. This notification was the only thing stopping the cleaning staff, or anyone else from the hotel, from crossing the threshold into their sanctuary.

Tolver kicked the door frantically and whispered, "Come on, guys! Open the door!" His impatience had him trotting around the hall as if he needed to use the restroom. Some of the items he was holding fell to the ground. When the door finally opened, he hit the hole like a running back, almost knocking Nathan into the wall.

Not pleased with the near miss, Nathan scolded him, "Hey, man, watch what you're doing!"

"Sorry, I didn't want to be seen carrying all this stuff."

Nathan's laugh mocked Tolver, "And what do you think they're going to do to you? It's not like you're running out the front door with it. We're staying here."

"I think you've become a little too comfortable with our situation. The whole point of our hiding is so we aren't seen. Even if we deserve this stuff, do they have to know we took it? Can't we just be anonymous?"

Rowen entered from one of the bedrooms and chimed in rather satirically, "You might be holding the only thing we can get away with stealing on this trip. You think Nathan having an alias like Luca Stashmire attached to this room is giving us some type of cover? As soon as the money goes missing from the safety-deposit box, he is sure to be the prime suspect. The man has been all over the hotel since we got here. The both of you even went to the Drake Room last night."

"Hey, we're here to celebrate his birthday. If I remember correctly, you endorsed us going to the Drake Room last night. By the way, they got a hell of a steak. Steak Nino, cooked in butter and wine with chives. Absolutely delicious," Nathan said with a prideful grin.

"Yeah, thanks for bringing us leftovers."

"If there were any, we would have brought them back."

Tolver was trying to put things on the counter. He wasn't having much success, which added to his agitation, and he chastised Nathan for it, "You're not helping the situation at all right now. Can you make yourself somewhat useful and go into the hall and bring in the stuff I dropped?"

Nathan bowed slightly as he turned to comply.

Not able to let go, Tolver also let Rowen know where he was at in the moment, "And yes, we went to the Drake Room last night, but I didn't feel comfortable the entire evening. We shouldn't be getting complacent, not as long as we're staying here. I mean, that's the point of renting this room, right?"

Slater had been lying on the couch the past few days in obvious discomfort. He struggled to raise his arm to let everyone know he had something to say. When he was acknowledged, he stated in a weak voice, "Staying here, not staying here, who gives a shit? I just want to know when we're going home?"

The room went quiet. Tolver thought he knew the answer but didn't want to say because he wasn't sure how to interpret the information.

Mallory had been in and out of consciousness since they arrived. It was clear the man was hurting. The moments where he was able to respond to their questions were few and far between. During these exchanges, they would soon discover he was hard of hearing. When Mallory was conscious, questions would have to be repeated more than once. This affliction wasn't as disturbing as his eyes. They seemed offset, somehow out of sync, as if one were lazy, giving their would-be guide a look as if he weren't altogether there.

When Mallory finally brought up the subject of their departure, he spoke of it only once. He told Tolver in the weakest of whispers that the trip would be over once they committed the heist. It didn't seem like much of an answer at the time, and it contradicted what they were told back at Tilt Time. Maybe this simplistic answer was all Mallory could get out in his weakened condition. He hadn't really thought about it much because of the other concerns that were weighing on him, like if they were going to have to go back to the Florentine to leave. Did they have to pack their supplies back into their cases? And how were they going to check out of this room without creating a bigger mystery?

Tolver thought they had already drawn enough attention when they moved Mallory and Slater to this suite. They had to prop both men up. Mallory was so weak he needed the support of a man under each of his long arms. They were a mess as they made a concerted push to their destination. The guests seemed uncomfortable as the group fumbled past them, treating them as if they were to be scorned for partying too hard the night before. One old couple quipped in disgust as they passed them, "Probably degenerates, here to see that hideous rock-and-roll band."

As far as the four of them were concerned, the hideous band had been put on hold. Tolver was more concerned with Mallory. His stretches of being comatose lasted a little longer each time he went under. As much as they all wanted to get him to a hospital, they thought it better to find another way of getting him help. Tolver believed they were caught up in a terrible trap with no way to remedy their situation. That was part of the reason the group sent him and Nathan to the Drake Room. It was a feeble attempt at giving them a break from the bleak state of affairs.

The door opened, and Nathan returned with the things Tolver had dropped. He made his way over to the credenza, "I think we have more than enough toilet paper."

With that comment, Tolver suddenly remembered what he was trying to accomplish before he stole the amenities. "Oh man, I forgot. I was heading to the Florentine to restock our supplies before I got distracted by the maid's cart at the other end of the hall."

Nathan shook his head and laughed, "No, no, no, birthday boy. You stay right here. I'll go down and fetch the things we need."

Upon hearing this, Tolver reached into his pocket and tossed Nathan the keys to the conference room. With keys in hand, Nathan was out the door in the blink of an eye.

Rowen was dismayed by what just happened, "See what I mean? That bastard has been out there roaming around more than he's been in here. Now you tell me, how's that keeping a low profile?"

Tolver sat down and put his head in his hands. He knew Nathan had been out in the hotel more than he should have. Their pony betting friend regaled him about the people he had met while on his excursions during dinner last night—a bartender at Sheppard's, a bellhop, even a roadie who spoke of a doctor the tour manager had put on standby at the hotel. Nathan boasted that the manager had hired the doctor due to the exhaustion the members of the band had been feeling during their tour. Since hearing about the doctor, Nathan had been on the prowl for the physician. He figured it would be quite a coup if he could somehow find and convince this medical professional to come back to their suite. So, Tolver was privy as to why Nathan had been wandering around the hotel, but he didn't want to cause any undue panic in the others by spilling the reason for this.

As Tolver tried to unwind, he realized he still had the paper under his arm. He opened the folded-up rag to reveal the front page of *The New York Times,* and he saw the motto: *All the News That's Fit to Print.*

The first thing that struck him was how toned down and tame the stories were from this era compared to the one he came from. The headlines weren't screaming about radicalized domestic terrorists, acts of partisan revenge, mass migration, countries ravaged by plagues, global scale pollution, or poverty so widespread it drove populations to lash out in the extreme. The reporting resonated as if humanity still cared—cared enough to try to contain the evil and tyranny gripping its ranks.

Rowen plopped down next to Tolver and slapped his knee, snapping him out of his read. Pulling his head out of the newspaper, Tolver responded, somewhat agitated, "What is it now?"

"Forget about Nathan. He can be a real putz sometimes. I got something better to tell you. You and me, we are going to tonight's show."

"What are you talking about? The concert?"

"Yes, I mean the concert. We've come too far not to go."

Tolver stood and walked across the room. With everything going on, he was trying to think how they were going to slip away. Rowen sensed his hesitation and tried to get him to loosen up.

"Hey, look. This is why we came. Only we were supposed to get three nights—concerts, parties, and, on top of it, knocking the place over. Well, we know two of those things ain't happening. So, that leaves us with the concert. What do you think? It would sure give us something to talk about the next time we are back at the bar chatting it up with Blake."

"And what? We just walk away from all this? Last night's outing was nerve-racking enough for me, and we were still in the hotel."

"Look, I can't make you go, but this is why we came, right? I mean, we took time off work and blew cash we really didn't have to see this concert."

"At Madison Square Garden," Tolver said, putting things into perspective.

"Hell yes, New York City, 1973, in Madison Square Garden. And not just any old band, but Led Zeppelin, five albums deep into their prime."

Tolver nodded slowly, "We're supposed to be there."

"Yes, we're supposed to be there, three times over. I think if we go one of the nights, just one, we won't be doing anyone a disservice."

Slater, who was supine on the couch, suddenly spoke up, "Please go, get him out of our hair. He's driving us all crazy."

Rowen immediately piped up, "Who? Me? Or do you mean Tolver?"

"You. You never shut up. At least with you gone, we'll have some peace and quiet around here."

"Well, look who woke up, mister grumpy." Rowen went to give Slater a hard time, but Tolver saw how much the man was suffering and reeled Rowen back in.

He spoke softly to Slater's antagonist and got him to stop, "Leave him be. If you want me to go tonight, then leave him be."

Rowen nodded and headed off to another room.

Tolver watched Slater doze back to sleep, still in obvious pain. Sitting there, he thought about how neither Mallory nor Slater would recover on their own. Tolver couldn't help but wonder how it was all supposed to end.

CHAPTER EIGHTEEN

CRASH CORDS AND KILL SWITCHES

Boone was making his way to the containment facility to initiate the final process for sending him on his next mission. This part of the plant was housed deep within the old STAR detector and was the last stop an explorer or marshal would make before heading to their locker. Deep within this structure was an isolated room, the containment facility, where a person would be as physically close to Landau as they would ever get. Within this room, a traveler would receive their last scan. Each bone, organ, and artery were given cardinal points that were logged and mapped. All the previous medical scans were matched up and fused together to create the traveler's Adinkra. This final scan ensured the quality of the packet and the security that the right human was being delivered into history.

The cardinal points were the cornerstones of rebuilding a person correctly on the other side. It was stated that a traveler wouldn't miss a heartbeat in the process. Sadly, Boone knew firsthand how untrue this was. Some of the botched rebuilds were horrific, and he couldn't zap them out of existence fast enough.

While Landau completed the final scans, the computer would uncover the digital key needed for sending a person down the appropriate entanglement corridor. The independent code was the key to unlocking the timeline of history in a daughter universe, but there is a catch. Humans could only go back to where people had already been. For instance, a traveler couldn't go to an alternate timeline where the dinosaurs never became extinct. From the moment they survived extinction, this alternative dinosaur existence was off-limits to a person. There were rumors the scientists studying these events would bump up against several alternate timelines like this, and all of them were devoid of humanity. Time was a tesseract. It was deeper and more robust than anyone could have ever imagined. Layers upon layers of grids crisscrossing each other, stretching across the expanse of eons but never touching, and with humankind carving out its own small niche.

Boone entered the industrial corridors of the building, proceeding until he got to the heavily guarded security checkpoint. Passing through a maze of turnstiles and one-way revolving doors was a game of chutes and ladders—you never knew when a gate would close and you'd be locked in. The penalty for being penned in meant one would be admitted for additional evaluation. These supposed random collars funneled an individual into a series of tests ranging from the physical to the psychological. Even as a marshal, he wasn't sure what those running the checkpoint were looking for, but whatever it was seemed deeper than this system of trap doors could contain.

Once through the security precautions, Boone took a long elevator ride down to his destination. He could never confirm just how far underground he had gone, though it was far enough that his ears popped. He would always spend the last few minutes forcefully yawning and working his jaw to get his ears back to equilibrium.

Stepping inside the high-tech lift, the elevator was in freefall and rattled like a carnival ride. He would always try and stand in the middle, not wanting to hold onto the rail. If he did, the vibrations from the car would travel from the handle, through his arm, until his whole body was shaking as if he had a chill. Just as he approached a point of genuine concern in the descent, the governor would kick in, bringing the cabin to a gradual stop.

Very few people on the planet would ever get to be within this close proximity of Landau. Of those he knew within the department who did, they approached the opportunity with a solemn demeanor—as if they were gaining access to something sacred. Boone's expectations were more on the uneasy side as if he were going to be judged.

He acknowledged being evaluated was an odd reaction to have in this situation. It was impossible for Landau to communicate directly. There were only prerecorded greetings and prompts—nothing that could ever be confused with having an actual conversation. Still, stories were circulating around campus about Landau reaching out and doing just that. To Boone, the stories were farfetched and fabricated. As far as he was concerned, they were told by those looking to gain attention. In all the times he had been down at that deep scanner, he had never experienced that type of interaction with Landau—nor did he know of anyone in his department who had. His attitude in situations involving Landau was to tread lightly and not screw it up.

He believed human error was always at the heart of any technological mishap. In his mind, anything a person could point to as an example of a malicious machine failed to see the egregious human interaction behind such a mistake. Bots, smart weapons, and autonomous vehicles all had humans assembling the operational infrastructure. They were launched by people. The machines were only acting on the information provided.

Down in that lair, the air was stale. They did their best to circulate it at this depth, but there was nothing fresh about the substance. He didn't care how many filters they ran it through, it still smelled manufactured, as if somebody dumped an old bottle of cleaner in the backroom.

The prerecorded welcome greeted him, and Boone responded, "Marshal 2969, reporting for final scan and assignment."

To ensure no marshal had any influence on their undertaking, the missions were picked randomly. This was done in the vein of keeping each marshal focused on their task of protecting history.

"Proceed," Landau's prerecorded voice echoed in the hallowed chamber.

Boone placed his hand on the touch-sensitive screen. A light bar slowly moved across his hand, reading the print. He stared into the retinal scanner and waited for Landau to begin his body survey.

With all this available technology at its disposal, Boone could not push himself past having suspicions of

Landau. If there was one machine that could think for itself, this was it. Landau was gathering information at a breakneck speed on every person who came here. At the same time, the technicians working within this area were rumored to be closed off from gaining access to the information field generator. Boone knew that voicing his concerns about this would be frowned upon by his superiors. Doubt in the program was usually cast by an explorer or a physicist. It was to be expected as those two groups would examine circumstances to the nth degree.

One rarely found a marshal wrapped in the robes of scientific discoveries. A project such as time travel seemed to uncover a new set of circumstances on any given week, like that of the sevatron. The news spread through the time travel community of this tiny oscillating particle made up of vibrating strings. Each string supposedly represented a dimension completely alien to this universe. It was hypothesized that Landau might be using these entangled strings to deposit a traveler back in time. Those who considered themselves part of the intellectual sect would spend countless hours poring over the information being churned out at Brookhaven regarding this new particle. They looked at things like its Planck energies, its reach into higher dimensions, its association with dark matter and the axion, and all the while tried to unlock exactly how Landau was utilizing it.

On the other hand, a marshal was more interested in what it took, day in and day out, to protect the projection of time. His side of the industry wasn't getting caught up in the shadow world of quantum mechanics—of everything having a dual meaning. For the marshals, this process didn't lean toward science; it fell more toward a singularity that was the letter of the law. So, it was disorienting for Boone to think that those in charge were basing their historical research on traveling back to any one of these multiple daughter universes. They were bubbles, countless numbers of bubbles. When viewed as a whole, they probably looked like a bathtub full of soap bubbles.

Boone couldn't detect a difference when in one of these stable realms—everything for him seemed the same. This was probably why those running the program approved the delivery of either a tourist or an explorer to yesteryear.

Much to his dismay, there were reports of daughter universes where explorers spoke of noticeable differences. Some were environmental or social distinctions, while others revealed a peculiar timeline not readily found anywhere else in their searches. They had reports showing a daughter universe where President Kennedy wasn't assassinated, and because of this, the government's involvement in Vietnam was constrained. They found one that reflected Alan Turing's computer not breaking the German enigma codes and World War II lasting much longer than anyone could have imagined. There was even a universe where the nation was broken, in decay, and run by a Sino-foreign adversary set on treating its denizens like second-class citizens.

In these universes, where things unfolded in such glaring contrast, those in charge of the program were trying to deduce the reasons for the drastic dissimilarities and how an explorer could end up there in the first place. Boone saw it differently; he didn't think the universes these explorers were sent to were accidents. He wondered if Landau was sending explorers to those alternate realities to test how far the information field could push things. It was a gut feeling, maybe he was basing it on how adamantly those scientists defended their creation, always looking to excuse the information field generator rather than coming clean that Landau may have done something wrong.

His misgivings didn't stop him from accepting every assignment they threw at him. Boone fearlessly followed explorers back in time as they tried to complete their mission. He quietly tagged along with tourists on their travels. When a request came in from the department, he rabidly pursued the subjects targeted by his superiors for investigation. In most instances, he shadowed his marks to ensure they weren't in danger or breaking the rules. When it came to the internal probes, he put more effort into it— stalking those suspects as if he were a private investigator. At times, he was hellbent, as if he were saving the world.

Boone recently noticed there had been an uptick in internal investigations. He had even heard they were starting to tail entanglement engineers out in the field. It was getting to the point where no one was beyond suspicion. What if the rumors about Landau reaching out and making contact with some of the staff weren't exaggerations?

There was a slight rumble under his feet as the flow of fluorocarbon circulated far below. Boone had a thought—

cutting off this much-needed coolant might be the only way to stop Landau from becoming incorporated with other quantum computers. He wished they had installed a kill switch on the information field generator, much like they had done within the tunnels supporting the rings. If anyone ever got trapped in an energized tunnel when the rings were turned on, they could pull on a crash cord and stop it from ramping up. It seemed like such a mistake now; they should have considered a kill switch for that computer buried deep in that hole right from the start.

Boone suddenly realized where he was, just moments away from his final scan being registered. His hand still firmly placed on the screen reader. Usually, the placing of one's hand on this console triggered the scan for the rest of his body. Glancing around the room, he noticed the lights had dimmed, and with it, there was a constant low hum of energy. He stood there in silence and slowly peeled his hand off the reader. The lights and hum instantly ramped back up, and after a few moments, the screen confirmed his scan. It also alerted him to his next assignment. He would oversee four tourists from Tilt Time.

His wrist and hand tingled, turning numb as if the contact with the console had gone beyond the surface of the screen. Boone made a fist to regain feeling and brought his other hand up to support his ailing wrist. Standing there, he could not shake his suspicion that Landau knew precisely what he had been thinking.

CHAPTER NINETEEN

A REAL CON

O nly one man was still thinking about the heist. Nathan had walked past the front desk on more than one occasion, counting out his paces to the staircase, down the halls, and to their suite. Even if the staff found out a minute or two after the safety-deposit box had been broken into, he figured the last place they would think a person would run was back into the hotel. He was betting security would make their way down into the main lobby and blanket the street beyond the front doors.

To get to the room where the cash was, one had to move down the narrow side hall next to the check-in desk until it ended with a ninety-degree turn. Then it was several more steps until, on the right, was a locked door. The room with the safety-deposit boxes was located directly behind the solid wall of the check-in counter.

While walking around the hotel retrieving supplies from the Florentine and searching for the elusive doctor, Nathan mulled over how and when to pull this high-stakes caper off. While contemplating this, he could not get rid of the melodic piano playing of Cy Walter out of his head. Cy played the cocktail lounge of the Drake Room with his recall of show tunes both famous and forgotten. It had only been one night, but the lively playing, combined with the refined feel of the bar, had a distinct impact on his soul. Nathan had been dipped in the night, and his immersion into this exquisite high-end lifestyle was a signal to all the possibilities of this era. The more he walked the halls of the hotel, the more he convinced himself that staying here was his destiny. He just needed to pull off the feat of stealing the band's cash.

There was another indication for Nathan that this was meant to be. He had made a discovery, quite by accident, on the set of keys they had gotten from Mallory. Nathan noticed a key that looked an awful lot like the one he had obtained when he rented his safety-deposit box. It seemed impossible at first, but then Nathan wondered if part of Mallory's job was to plant this key for them to find later. That might mean one of the other keys opened the room, but he had to be sure. So, well before the sun rose the previous day and while everyone was still in bed, he snuck back to the Palm Court and made his way down the L-shaped hall to the door protecting the safety-deposit boxes. It didn't take long before he confirmed there was a key on the ring that did indeed open the door.

Pilfering this money was a charade. They didn't have to steal any keys as they were led to believe at the beginning of this adventure. Mallory had treated them like children, leading them on and creating tension when there was none to be had. Every question on this journey had already been answered. *Of course, it was; time was etched in stone!* Nathan stewed with the thought that Mallory, Carmichael, and everyone back at Tilt Time were nothing more than hucksters. Well, if they felt it within their rights to dupe them on this trip, then he had a surprise of his own in store. After

Tolver tossed him the key ring for the supplies in the Florentine, Nathan decided to keep them. Now that they were in his possession, Nathan would show those bastards back at Tilt Time what a real con looked like.

CHAPTER TWENTY

THE OCEAN

T he crowd at Madison Square Garden was electrified. They were getting boisterous as they clapped and shouted in anticipation of Led Zeppelin taking the stage. Both Tolver and Rowen witnessed the build of this frenetic energy as they walked to The Garden. The bumper-to-bumper traffic filled the air with a heavy, pungent exhaust as radio stations blared from the rolled-down windows of vehicles whose occupants were trying to stay cool in the heat of the city.

Street vendors, newsstands, and ticket scalpers shouted out their inventory and added to the building climate of festivities. Rowen was especially frisky that night, finally free from what he termed "the Drake penitentiary." He took full advantage, engaging with as many people as humanly possible along the way. He struck up conversations with fans, hugged them as if they were long-lost friends, and heartily partook in what they offered in smoke and drink. All the while, he kept trying to pull Tolver into this animated atmosphere. Finally, after enough egging on, and with the help of some joyous souls that included a few beautiful women, Tolver dropped his guard.

The blue tickets they flashed to the attendant took them to the orchestra section, floor level, twenty seats back from the band. As they filed in with the crowd, they could see the stage lit with soft, warm light. The roadies rushed around performing final checks. From their seats, they could see the fervor of players and groupies with backstage passes jockeying for position along the wings of the stage. The crowd clapped and cheered for what felt like an eternity while they waited for the band. No one dared to take a seat. Everyone was charged and excited as they waited for Pagey, Percy, Jonsey, and Bonzo. There were no opening acts; the audience would get what they had paid for—would see Led Zeppelin play from the first song to the last, in all their sonic glory.

Then, without warning, the lights went out. The crowd got loud—really loud. They cheered and hollered fanatically, their screams and shouts rising to the rooftop. In this roaring sea of sound, they waited for the band to take the stage until their collective voices came together as one. At peak crescendo, the band came out and took their positions. John Bonham began the concert by banging out the opening on his drums. It was the tumultuous beat of their song, "Rock and Roll." The lights did not come on until the blaze of guitars came in, and then the crowd reacted. Some shrieked, some threw things, others jumped, with everyone responding to the lit appearance of the four musicians.

The band was bathed in a fading haze from the canned blue, red, green, and yellow lights high above. Paige, with his golden locks flowing, moved back and forth to the beat in his skinny jeans and matching unbuttoned short blue shirt. Robert Plant was shredding his guitar. His black outfit was topped off with an unbuttoned jacket adorned with white stars, epaulets of gold, and a medieval orange dragon emblazoned on the back. The least animated of the band was John Paul Jones, who played his bass while standing off to the left of the drums, looking very cool in his colorful fringe suede jacket. John Bonham rocked out on the drums, complimented by his thick mustache and a headband that kept his long hair in check.

They performed knowing it was their last weekend of a long tour. Their smiles were genuinely relentless as they punched out their blues-rock brilliance. Tolver and Rowen took in the magic of every drumbeat and every lick of wailing guitars. They cheered with the audience between these extended boogie jams and clapped their hands raw.

Ending the concert on a high note, the band played "The Ocean." It was appropriate for the current of energy that had been swirling about the historic venue. It pulled the crowd in, along with Tolver and Rowen, with all the power of a riptide that swelled into a rogue wave of post-celebrations and parties.

This jubilation would last long into the morning for some and yield a lifetime of memories for others.

CHAPTER TWENTY-ONE

BLACK DOG

It was just before three in the morning when Nathan crept downstairs and into the lobby. He witnessed several intoxicated patrons at the front desk. The boisterous customers wanted to get some dancing in and one or two libations before allowing their night to end. This was the make-or-break point in Nathan's plan to grab the cash. The distraction was made to order as the only two staff members did their best to deal with the drunken commotion. While the backs of these two staff members were turned, Nathan slithered skillfully to the side of them and down the hall toward the locked door.

Everything was going smoothly until he made the turn down the small hallway. For some strange reason, his legs stiffened, and his breathing grew heavier. The walls began closing in on him, and the hall got longer. It was as if he would never be able to make it to the other end, but he fought to continue.

Beads of sweat broke out on his forehead as he pulled out a pair of stolen blue velvet gloves the valets wore on colder nights and put them on. His numb fingers searched through his pockets to find the ring of keys. Standing at the end of the hall, he leafed through the bunch to insert the correct one into the doorknob. This was it. Later, it would be reported in the papers that only those working the front desk had a key to get through this door, or so they thought. It truly was the perfect crime. Nathan smiled in anticipation and slowly opened the door.

Standing still for a moment, Nathan noticed how much cooler it was in this room. Chilled, he couldn't help but marvel in the moment, taking it all in. The doors to the safety-deposit boxes were located on two walls. The entire place was accented in a deep, rich brown, which met the plush, deep forest green carpet beneath his feet. In the center of it all was a large dark table, supported by two wooden slabs so a person could stand at it while going through the contents of their box.

It looked like the table they had waited at before departing Tilt Time. He wondered if the selection of that slab were purposeful, but his pondering was short-lived as he heard the commotion from the inebriated patrons at the front desk once again.

Nathan assumed the band's safety-deposit box would be one of the larger ones. The wall directly across from him was the only wall lined with large boxes. He looked at the keyring again and found the one he was convinced would open one of these larger panels. He started with the top row, and after trying the first five, the key suddenly slid into the lock and turned. Sweat ran down the side of his cheek as the door swung wide. He stood there and stared at the metal box inside. He wondered if the boxes were rigged to light up a bulb at the front desk when removed. He stared at the box as his mind worked overtime, playing with all the *what ifs*. Everything he needed for his new start in life was contained within that box, and it wouldn't be waiting for him forever.

He would only get this one chance—so, taking a deep breath, he reached up with his gloved hand, grabbed the handle, and slowly slid it out.

With the gunmetal-gray box free, he felt the weight of it. The heaviness told him he had hit pay dirt. Nathan was like a child anticipating the opening of a shiny wrapped gift. Setting it down, he began to claw at it with his gloved hands, trying to figure out how it opened. *Did the top slide? Did it pull out again like a drawer?* It took him a moment before he made out the two small hinges three-quarters down the top of the box. The lid bounced as it slipped from his hand, revealing the well of cash inside.

The bills were in stacks folded over on themselves. Each round wad was held together by rubber bands of various colors and widths. Trembling, Nathan reached into the box and grabbed the money. He placed it inside his jacket and pants pockets. When those filled, he had a small cloth laundry sack he had taken from their suite and began shoving the rest of the cash inside. When the safety deposit box had been emptied of money, he sucked in his gut and stuffed the bag into his pants.

Finished, he patted himself down to be sure his pockets weren't bulging too badly. Satisfied he appeared somewhat normal, he contemplated closing the box and replacing it. This made no sense to him, so he left things just as they were, made his way over to the door and slowly pulled it open. He peered around the jamb and down the hall. After closing the door behind him, he removed his gloves.

Nathan could hear a lively exchange as he made his way down the little hall toward the front desk. This time, someone was attempting to get a room, and the clerk was explaining that they were sold out. Peering around the corner, Nathan saw the clerk was sufficiently distracted with this guest, and he made a break for it.

His gait was wider than usual because he found himself walking much faster. Try as he might, Nathan could not hide the huge, ear-to-ear grin plastered across his face.

CHAPTER TWENTY-TWO

WHEN THE LEVEE BREAKS

V ance McMillan was the chief operations officer for the division, a seasoned, well-groomed, and polished individual who always seemed to have a consistent greasy sheen across his facial features. This was due to the skin treatments and lotions he used to maintain his clean-cut appearance. Perhaps when he was younger, those self-care practices personified his masculinity in a more positive light, but as the years wore on, they marked a distinctive retreat. The slick shine only seemed to accentuate the decaying collection of wrinkles and imperfections layered throughout his facial features. The two characteristics that never changed in any photograph ever taken of him—were the precise part in his hair and the knit of his eyebrows as they merged together, giving him a permanent look of concern.

No analyst in their right mind ever wanted to be alone with McMillan—let alone deliver unfavorable news to him—but that was exactly where Eugene Ballaster found himself. After gathering the last bit of information from the data control center, Eugene made his way to Vance's office as quickly as he could. When finally admitted, Eugene found McMillan seated behind his desk and staring oddly at him. His doll's eyes topped off the look of a crash test dummy strapped in just before the car was to be launched.

"Well, hit me with it. Don't pull any punches."

Eugene kicked the floor leaving a scuff mark. He

hated being the bearer of bad news, "It's a mess... That's what it is."

"I know that. My seven-year-old nephew could have told me that."

"Where to start? As of now, the tourists are in a comatose state. The comas were induced by the doctors over at Tilt Time until officials from our offices can get a handle on what has happened."

"They wouldn't have had to knock them out if they didn't rebuild them. Who authorized this? They could have kept those tourists on ice indefinitely, kept them locked in their Adinkras until we got positive control of the situation."

"For all the influence the government has over Tilt Time, it's still a commercial venture. The corporation was getting barraged with inquiries from the victims' families and friends. The press has been relentless as well, hounding the company about the status of the tourists. Not being able to produce pictures, videos, or even medical readouts of the bodies was a scrutiny they couldn't ignore. They had to rebuild the bodies, or it would look as if the company was part of a coverup."

"Because it is! By rebuilding them, it has taken the attention off their company and shone a light on our other problems."

"The missing tourist...? Surely Tilt Time can't be blaming that on us?"

"And bite the very hand that feeds them? I doubt it.

Without Landau, their whole operation, the entire franchise, would fall flat on its keister." McMillan took the time to rock back in his chair as he thought for a moment, "No... they were sidestepping by rebuilding those tourists. They were washing their hands of this situation."

"How's that?"

"By rebuilding them, they don't have to pull the plug. Tilt Time has fulfilled its requirements. The company has publicly reported that the tourists have made it back safely."

"But that's not true! Some are not doing so well, like their guide, Mallory."

"Which only adds to my argument that Tilt Time is washing their hands of anything to do with them. Why would they go through the trouble of rebuilding as is, so injured and hurt? You and I both know those medical labs have the capability to rebuild tourists undamaged—in fact, even better than before they left. Hell, we do it all the time."

"Oh my god, you're right!"

"They rushed through the process, rebuilding them as is, so they could put it in the books that those tourists officially made it back to the present. It's reckless, and it lobs any further problems from here on out in our direction."

"That makes no sense. Some of their own people are suffering."

"It makes perfect sense because now they can report to the press and their detractors that these men didn't fare well. People will naturally associate this was due to the blast."

"They can report on all but one, and that's another problem."

"That is correct. One of them went missing."

"According to Tilt Time, he never returned."

"No Eugene, no. We can't let that kind of story out into the mainstream. We need to convince the public this tourist was lost in the explosion."

"And how are we going to go about doing that?"

"The surviving tourists are one problem. That's for sure. Tilt Time blew an opportunity to have a narrative inserted into their memory that would have been in line with what we needed to clean this up. Having missed one opportunity, we can start with another. The entanglement engineer, Julianne Bobrick. Isn't she being accused of setting this whole mess into motion?"

"That's the claim."

"That's a hell of a claim. Which agency is saying that?"

"It doesn't matter who said it. I've personally remedied the situation."

"You've personally remedied it?"

"Yes."

"Yeah, well, you can get a little more personal and find out what happened to Nathan Daugherty. We can't have Tilt Time talking about him as if he is still alive and wandering around in 1973."

"Yes, well, we've looked into him. Nathan has a rather colorful past. You could say he was a grifter at heart. He currently has a bookie howling for his blood. The man claims Tilt Time is purposely hiding Nathan."

"He can't mean Tilt Time is refusing to rebuild him, can he? I thought the public was completely unaware of that part of the process."

"They are. The rebuilding process is not a selling feature. As you know, upon being rebuilt, they are incapacitated and placed in pods. When they wake up, the tourist thinks they arrived in the pod. It's for their own well-being."

"So, you're telling me a bookie is convinced Tilt Time is hiding this guy. They deny it, but this same company isn't willing to do a second rebuild on these tourists to save the reputation of this industry?"

"You want them to switch them out."

"All we need is for Nathan's friends to say he was lost in the blast."

"We haven't seen the data from the trip to know whether that is even plausible or not."

"Wait a minute. We don't have copies of their Adinkras?"

"Not since we found out they had been rebuilt. No one saw the need to possess the information."

"No one saw the need?! Damnit, Eugene, I want the data on the tourists' Adinkras sent over immediately for review. We have no idea what they experienced, who they met, or what their state of mind will be like once revived. Who was the marshal assigned to this trip?"

"Boone Masterson. It seems the explosion influenced his portion of the mission as well."

"How is that possible? He left from this institution."

"Well, we aren't quite sure. He was gone for the appropriate length of time, but it appears he never reached his destination."

"You mean to tell me those bastards back in '73 weren't being monitored by a marshal?"

"That's correct. They had no oversight whatsoever."

"The oversight committee is not going to like hearing that."

"I'm afraid there's more. They are holding Boone's data in the system, waiting on approval to rebuild him. His scans aren't matching up."

"There is no way to make an exact copy of anything. Those are the laws of physics. Hell, these marshals and explorers have bounced down the entanglement corridors so many times; none of their scans will ever completely match up."

"Yes, but his scans aren't matching up in ways they haven't seen before. His organs have been altered ever so slightly. The medical staff told me they wouldn't even have looked at his data this closely if it wasn't for the explosion at Tilt Time. The doctors wanted to be thorough in their evaluation, so they bypassed the system safeguards and did a deep pass of their own. What they got back was completely unexpected—an Adinkra close to being Boone, but one that clearly *isn't* Boone."

"Wait a minute. You're telling me Landau is giving them the green light to rebuild, but the medical staff pulls the handbrake on the operation and checks into it themselves and finds unacceptable inadequacies?"

"I know it's very irregular, but it's not Landau's fault."

"Not his fault? The damn thing has been approving rebuilds for God knows how long, and we're just finding out now that they haven't been meeting the standards of a random scan the medical staff might give? I thought they had programmed Landau to attain the deepest scans possible?"

"Apparently, the issue is within its internal settings. The lower standard was something they had for their baseline tests when they were sending monkeys and dogs across campus."

"But that was years ago."

"I know, and as things progressed, they never took those lines of code out. The technicians are still trying to complete the system audit but released a report on their initial findings a couple of hours ago. According to those findings, anytime the system compared the scans of an explorer and found a discrepancy, it reverted to that original line of code using the old baseline and would greenlight the rebuild."

"You mean to tell me every rebuild we have done hasn't met the highest achievable standards the committee issued when we first began sending people through it?"

"They had different goals back then; they were trying to impress elected officials for more funding."

"Monkeys and mutts! That's been our high bar?"

"The medical staff is scrambling to answer that. They have a team combing through the records of our rebuild history, but it looks as of right now... we haven't met those standards."

"My God, we've been rebuilding people who might have been compromised in some way."

"Compromised?"

"Yes, their immune system, their mental faculties, physical ailments... Can we even be sure who these people are?"

Eugene found himself not wanting to say another word about the situation, but perhaps this conjecture helped to explain why some explorers or marshals were having difficulties adapting upon their return. The medical staff had attributed these symptoms to the rigors of traveling through time, but maybe there was a more compelling reason. It was quite possible that some of the people they rebuilt didn't belong in this universe. As the silence grew, so did the glaring problem of their missing marshal.

McMillan uttered what was becoming the crux of this catastrophe, "So, where's Boone?"

CHAPTER TWENTY-THREE

WHAT IS AND WHAT SHOULD NEVER BE

Tolver and Rowen, both blitzed from the night's festivities, stumbled back to their suite early in the morning. They quietly snickered as they passed a snoring Slater and a slumbering Nathan, who had both crashed on the couches. They headed to the only room left, the other being occupied by Mallory. They argued for several minutes about who would sleep in the rollaway bed. This was how they ended their long night out on the town after seeing Led Zeppelin.

They started the new day with a persistent knocking on the door. Slater annoyingly called out from the living room for someone to answer it. After enough nagging, Tolver summoned the energy to roll out of bed. He hit the floor, feeling woozy and weak. The bright light of day streaming in through the windows was like shots from a ray gun, blinding Tolver and stifling any chance he had of a quick rebound. The night of partying had taken its toll. With his hands raised to shield his eyes, he zig-zagged his way down the hall, past where Slater was still laid up, and toward the incessant rapping on the door, "Who is it?"

"It's Nathan. Open the damn door."

Tolver couldn't believe what he was hearing. He responded by giving him an earful after letting him in, "Have you gone mad? Why do you keep leaving the room without your key? Next time, you can stay out there for all I care."

Nathan walked past him, sporting his Cheshire grin, "You don't mean that."

"Yes, I do. You defy everything we are supposed to be doing on this trip. Why is it I feel we'll be the ones having to answer for it?"

Nathan grabbed a bottle of seltzer water from the wet bar. Popping the cap with an opener, he took a huge swig. Afterward, he used his sleeve to wipe his mouth. "Each of us will have to answer for what we've done. There's no doubt about that."

Tolver let the door close and staggered over to Nathan, "If you're implying we did something wrong, you can shove that implication up your ass."

"It's not for me to say."

There was another knock at the door.

Both Tolver and Nathan looked at each other. Nathan interjected, "Well, at least you know it isn't me." Nathan then turned to answer it, "Who's there?"

"Doctor Grimble."

Nathan opened the door wide, "Doctor Grimble, how good of you to come by."

"Well, the band still hasn't returned from their night on the town, so I thought I'd drop by to see what all the fuss was about."

"Come in. Come in."

Doctor Grimble walked into the untidy room and saw

Slater passed out on the couch in a sweat-stained T-shirt and wrinkled jeans. Nathan pointed to Slater, "That's one of them."

Grimble gestured toward the hungover Tolver. "I'm assuming that peaked-looking gentleman is the other?"

"No, no. You can ignore him; he's just a victim of last night's concert."

Grimble looked Tolver over and then back to Nathan, "I don't know if I can, Mr. Stashmire. I've made the house call. I might as well take care of everyone while I'm here."

"Right, right. Heaven knows we need it." Nathan glanced at Tolver, who in return waited for the doctor to look away before he mockingly mouthed the name Mr. Stashmire.

Nathan crossed the room and kicked the couch, "Alvarez, wake up." When he got no response, Nathan reached down and nudged him, "Alvarez, wake up. The doctor is here."

Having been awoken in this fashion, Slater begrudgingly responded, "What the hell are you saying? Alvarez? Leave me alone."

Nathan laughed and shook him again, "C'mon, buddy, I know you're hurting, but the doctor has finally come by to see you."

Agitated, Slater rolled over onto his side, "Doctor? What doctor?"

"Alvarez, this is Doctor Grimble. He's come to have a look at you."

Slater saw a tall, well-dressed gentleman in a dark blue suit, holding a black leather medical bag. He wore a stethoscope around his neck in the usual fashion of a medical professional.

As Doctor Grimble conversed with Slater about his condition, Nathan made his way back to Tolver, who looked stunned, "You brought a doctor to our room?"

"Well, what else were we going to do? Nobody wanted to take Slater or Mallory to the emergency room, so here we are."

"But isn't this going to blow our cover? I mean, the hotel sending a doctor will certainly draw attention, especially after this guy sees how bad off Mallory is."

"The hotel didn't send him. This is the doctor for the band. He came up here per my request. He'll be totally discreet, but it goes without saying, it's for a price."

"Discreet? You can't be sure of that."

"That's exactly what I can be sure of. I'm paying for just that."

They both glanced over to see Slater standing as best he could with his T-shirt raised to expose his left side and back. One large, deep bruise started at his hip and worked its way up past his ribs. The center of this was black and blue, but as it radiated out, it turned into blotchy patches of yellow and purple. Seeing him in this state hurt Tolver, giving him phantom pains. The doctor had him lower his shirt and sit back down. He dug in his bag, then handed Slater a pill. After watching him take it, he made his way over to Tolver and Nathan.

"Well, what's the verdict, Doc?"

"Not good. Whatever happened to him won't heal on its own. He's got a deep contusion, possibly some bruised or broken ribs. It's difficult to say. He should be taken to a hospital for X-rays and observation. I've given him a painkiller that should last for several hours; that's how much time you have to get him to a hospital. If you don't, you will most certainly have to send for an ambulance."

"Got it."

"You said there were two individuals. Where is our second patient?"

"In the next room." Nathan led him down the hall to Mallory. The room was dimly lit. It was mid-afternoon but the shades were drawn. The doctor asked for the window to be opened so the place could be aired out. Nathan was perplexed by the request. He didn't think it was possible to open a window in their suite. After making his way over, he raised the blinds, and much to his surprise, unlatched the window and lifted it to allow a breeze into the room. Grimble asked for the door to be left open and for Nathan to leave.

When Doctor Gimble finally emerged from the room, his suit jacket was off, and the sleeves of his expensive buttoned shirt were rolled up. He made his way over to Nathan.

"I propped him up and put a cold compress on his

neck and forehead. Leave the window open and keep getting air into this place. I gave him a shot of antibiotics, but that's as far as I'll go. For as long as you say he's been out, I wouldn't give him any amphetamines—he is well beyond that. I know you wanted them both to be treated here, but after seeing them, you need to get them to the emergency room as soon as possible."

"There's no other way?"

"Without proper medical attention, they will only get worse."

The doctor opened his bag and pulled out a few vials with dropper tops, small bottles of pills, and a black mortar and pestle. "You guys look like you could use a boost," he said as he began making his special vitamin concoction.

A boost? Tolver stood there for a moment, thinking about what the doctor had just said. It reminded him of something he noticed after they had arrived—when he was finally able to take his first shower. The bandage he should have had on his arm for his booster shot was gone. He had never removed it and wondered what its absence could possibly mean. He tried hard to recall. In his weakened, hungover mind, there was a horrific visual flash of him strapped inside a pod, struggling to break free, and then the grinding of the pestle in the mortar brought him back to what was happening in the hotel room.

"Don't forget to include ..." Tolver had to think for a moment, *What did it say on Rowen's driver's license?* "... ah, Cedric."

"Oh yeah, we got one more victim from last night's concert in the other room."

"Okay, I'll make three, but afterward, get both those men to the emergency room."

Tolver, quietly panicking, whispered, "What are we going to do? We can't take Mallory to the hospital."

Nathan waved him off, "We'll figure it out. Let me take care of the doctor first."

After a few moments, Doctor Grimble had three small paper cups with black liquid sitting on the wet bar. "Alright, Mr. Stashmire, that should do it—unless, of course, I can fix something else up for you?"

Nathan handed him a wad of cash. "I appreciate that, but it won't be necessary."

As they walked toward the door, the doctor gave him one last bit of advice, "Take a little of the vitamin cocktail and rub it on your two friends' gums. That should help in getting them up and to the hospital."

They shook hands, and before Tolver could blink, the doctor was gone.

"Well, that's great. Now we gotta get Mallory to the hospital sometime today."

"I didn't bring the doctor up here to tell us what we already knew." Nathan walked over to the wet bar and leaned against it, exhausted.

"Well, then, why did you invite him?"

"For this." He referenced the three shots sitting on the bar.

Tolver shook his head in disbelief, "I don't understand…"

"This will provide the spark we need to get this crew back down to the Florentine. The sooner, the better. I mean, look at this place. We are on the verge of living in squalor."

Tolver looked around and had to agree with him. He grabbed one of the paper cups, acknowledging Nathan. "When you're right, you're right. We gotta get outta here." With that, he knocked back the bitter-tasting shot, making a horrible face.

CHAPTER TWENTY-FOUR

D'YER MAKER

J ulianne had waves of guilt ever since her meeting with Eugene. To make matters worse, there was always a news story that mentioned the explosion playing wherever she went.

She had been quietly serving out her suspension from the entanglement engineer program, working in the quantum data division. First, she would comb over the equations the information field generator churned out in response to a scientific inquiry. Then, after reviewing them, she would catalog the data for the physicists to go over later. Those mathematical formulas were long and drawn out, and one would grow weary trying to comprehend them, but that didn't stop Julianne from trying. She was hoping within those lines, there would be a message from Landau— something that would be the proof she needed to be reinstated in the engineering corps.

Occasionally, she would have to submit to a drug test, a written exam, or a full body scan. This may have been to keep her on the up and up, but it also telegraphed to her that they were still interested in keeping her in the program.

She yearned to return to the gritty world of collecting particles. She was hopeful she would once again go out on missions that did more than just cross state lines. She loved having a job only a few people on the planet could do. She was addicted to going undercover and crossing international boundaries, peppered with pockets of danger and, in the end, feeling as if she were making a difference. For those reasons, she never questioned when or where they needed her to be on campus, but in hindsight, maybe she should have.

She was making her way to a containment facility located just off the Tandem Van de Graaff center. They had converted this abandoned structure to repair the bio-printers used to rebuild the travelers after returning from their trips. It was an odd place to have a meeting to reinstate her in the entanglement engineer program, but that's where they told her to meet. She was too excited to think it through.

Her first inclination that something was amiss was when Eugene finally greeted her with some of his suited goons in tow.

"Surprised to see me here, Julianne?"

"I don't understand. Am I in more trouble?"

"Why would you think that? Have you done something wrong?"

"No. Seeing you here, I just assumed."

Eugene turned and began walking deeper into the building. "Do you know what they do in this structure? They fix the machines that rebuild the explorers and marshals. These bio-printers must be gone over and fined-tuned all the time. The slightest error can create all kinds of difficulties and delays in a rebuild. I've seen some botched rebuilds; not an accident anyone should see, they are not pretty. To keep on top of things, the technicians bring those machines here, swap them out, tear them apart, rework them until they function like new again."

As she followed along, she could see the employees in white coveralls going over the machines in a well-lit, open area, but that's not where they were headed. Eugene turned and began walking to a dark, remote part of the building that smelled of burnt electricity.

"This place never sleeps, operating day and night. I hear combined, there are enough bio-printers that we could pump out over a few hundred people at a time. That's pretty incredible when you think about it. I've often wondered how they test the machines before they put them back into service."

"I don't understand how this has anything to do with me being reinstated?"

"Oh, but you will."

Julianne followed Eugene into a secure room. The lights flickered and came to life when they entered. Julianne saw a bio-printer humming on the other side of the room. Although she had never seen one in action, this machine appeared to be working on a person.

Getting closer, she peered through the observation window and saw a woman. The entity glistened in the sealed environment and looked exactly like herself. Startled, she swung around to confront Eugene, "What the hell is this?"

"I'll admit, if I saw myself in there, I'd probably have the same reaction. It's a little unorthodox, but this is how we will get you back into the program."

"You think you can revive that thing and send it out on missions? You're mad. How will she even know what to do out in the field?"

"That thing is *you*, Julianne, right down to how you blink, eat, think, and recite poetry. It will know exactly what to do out in the field once we send her there, trust me. As of right now, you are one of our most valued assets in the engineering program, and the funny thing is, if anything ever happened to you out in the field, we could simply rebuild another."

"That's insane! You'll never get away with it."

"But we already have. She's very close to being finished, ready to step up and take your spot within the program. There is just one problem. We can't have two versions of you running around doing the same job and living the same life."

"What are you talking about? She has no training. You think she will just be able to walk right into the Special Collections Branch?"

"She knows everything you know, maybe even more."

"And you trust that thing enough to get rid of me? You're out of your mind!"

"No, I'm not. We have a whole industry that disposes of travelers' remains all the time. A crematorium that operates around the clock. Who would question the body of one more?"

Julianne backed away but was stopped by the two goons in suits. Eugene smiled broadly, "You know, if the information is spliced just right with this rebuild, the new you might not find me so repulsive. On the contrary, I will even venture to say you would find me… quite desirable."

Julianne fought to contain her fury, "Look at me. Whatever you do with these other versions, you'll never truly be with me. There is nothing remotely desirable about you."

"Why would you say that? Can't you see I'm giving you one last chance to come around?"

"And be with you? You're hideous. I'm nauseated by the very sight of you! A pungent, disgusting pig of a man. Never!"

Eugene approached as Julianne's rage continued to build, struggling against her captors, she drew her head back and spit at Eugene. The wad stopped him in his tracks. It stuck to his face like bird shit on a windshield. In response, Eugene calmly pulled the gun from his shoulder holster, stepped back, and pointed it at her.

The technicians who heard the gunshot reverberate through the building thought it was just one of the many loud reactions of the metallic hydrogen within the rings of the Relativistic Heavy Ion Collider.

CHAPTER TWENTY-FIVE

BABE, I'M GONNA LEAVE YOU

A n uptight Tolver busily went about packing cases down in the Florentine. There was so much stuff that had gone untouched, like the backpacks they should have carried with them, the water purification pills, and the food they were supposed to be eating. It was all still here, jumbled about in their respective cases as they rummaged for other items they needed, like toilet paper. The realization of this unused stockpile was only part of the problem. He had spent the better part of the day getting everyone from the suite into the conference room. They were helped by an unexpected commotion taking hold of the hotel, and Tolver wanted to know more about it, "So, did you ever find out what all the hubbub was about?"

Rowen, carrying two bags with the groups' personals and clothing, deposited them with the rest of the stuff and responded excitedly, "There are cops everywhere downstairs. I heard the FBI has shown up."

"Why?"

"I guess it has something to do with the robbery."

"Robbery? You mean of Led Zeppelin? How is that possible? We didn't do it."

"I don't know, but somebody did. Maybe the people who were actually supposed to do it. I heard they tried to lock the place down and do room searches. But the police never made it past the lower floors. Roadies were breaking back into the hotel and then into their rooms to flush away all their drugs."

"That's insane."

"That's what one of the bellhops told me. He said some of his pals were letting the roadies in. I even heard two guys were smuggled back into the hotel in a laundry hamper."

"Well, it's a good thing we moved when we did. I mean, it took a lot out of Slater and Mallory even after their little vitamin boost."

"Precisely, and not a moment too soon." Nathan was finishing stuffing plastic bags of garbage they had accumulated into one of the cases.

'Thank you, Doctor Grimble," Rowen said, putting his hands together as if praying.

Tolver nodded, "Yeah, man, that was a great pinch. Definitely helped in getting Slater and Mallory down here."

"So now what?" Nathan asked from across the room.

"Now what, what?" Tolver didn't understand Nathan's question.

"Are we supposed to arrange ourselves in a certain order, a pattern of some sort? The gear? Us? How does this all work for the return?"

Tolver paused. It had been well over two days ago, but it felt more like eons. He couldn't bring himself to mention his recent nightmarish visual of struggling inside the pod. He responded as if to erase the torment. "To be honest, I don't even remember how we got here."

Rowen piped up, "We were in that room with the narrow table talking with Carmichael. Remember? He was passing out our wallets and tickets."

"That's right, the assembly area." Nathan said this as if recalling a dream.

"Yeah, but I don't remember having to be in any particular order." Tolver said.

"Neither do I." Rowen with a broad smile.

"Then it's set." Nathan made it sound as if they finalized a deal.

"We made it!" Tolver gave Rowen two thumbs up and matched it with a broad smile.

Nathan volunteered, "Great! I'll go up and check the room one last time to make sure it's clear of our stuff."

"Perfect. Rowen and I will go back over the cases to make sure they're all secure."

Nathan stood there for a moment, surveying the room before he turned and left.

After the door closed, Rowen asked, "What are we going to do when we are finished here?"

"What? You wanna dine at the Drake Room as well?" Tolver looked at him incredulously.

"Naw, I was thinking about hanging out by The Garden. We have the tickets and one more night ahead of us. Maybe we can find another party," Rowen winked.

"Yeah, well, whatever it is, it's gotta be on the cheap. We didn't rob the band. What little money we have left in our wallets is counterfeit."

"Just think if the cops came in here. What would they make of all of this?"

Tolver stopped to examine the situation, "It doesn't look good, that's for sure. Gotta hand it to those guys back at Tilt Time, though—safe houses, fake IDs, the clothing… I mean, with everything going on out there, I feel like we could explain ourselves."

Laid out on his back, Slater raised his arm to get their attention. Recognizing this, Tolver made his way over and knelt beside him. Slater's arm fell onto Tolver's shoulder, and he pulled Tolver closer, then spoke in a weakened state, "He's got it."

"What? Who's got what?"

"He's got the money."

"Nathan?" Tolver said in shock as Slater nodded.

"I saw him. I saw him hide it." That was all Slater said before he passed out again.

Tolver looked over to Rowen, who had only heard a portion of the conversation, "He saw who?"

"Slater said he saw Nathan with the money from the

safety-deposit box."

"What? The band's money? Are you sure?"

"I don't know. I mean, he paid Doctor Grimble with a wad of cash. I didn't think too much of it at the time. I was more concerned with Mallory and Slater."

"You think he's going to try to spend it all tonight… by himself?"

Tolver's stomach turned over in knots. It always did when things began to spiral out of control, "No. I don't think he's going to spend it."

"He's not coming back, is he?"

"I don't know… In my gut, I guess I do. The man is crazy." There was a moment of silence as Tolver gathered his thoughts. There was no getting around it. Every step of the way with Nathan, he had been taken advantage of—totally played. He finally blurted out, "We gotta stop him."

"What? You mean, the both of us?"

"No. I'll do it." Tolver gave Rowen a matter-of-fact look, "You gotta stay here and look after the guys. I'll go."

Rowen patted Tolver's shoulder as he stood and headed for the door.

Once out in the oversized level of the mezzanine, Tolver retraced his steps to the Palm Court. It was a hunch, but he felt by the time he got up to the suite, Nathan would already be on his way down. Tolver's best bet was to wait and see if he could catch Nathan in the lobby.

When Tolver stepped into the Palm Court, he had the sensation of being in another world. Here was a place where people understood their purpose in life and moved faster than he could ever move. Perhaps his caution for this situation came from all the law enforcement activity around the check-in desk.

The cops had their suspicions based on the fact that nothing was broken into, so it looked like an inside job. They were focusing their attention on the band managers and hotel staff. This was the main reason the room searches had ceased, and the hotel guests were allowed to move about freely.

A crowd of fans, groupies, news reporters, and photographers gathered in the lobby to catch a glimpse of the band returning to the hotel. Of course, they were aware of the robbery. It may have been why Page, Plant, Jones, and Bonham had stayed away for so long—hoping the energy would have died down. Instead, the pressure was building, as if against the walls of a submarine the deeper it went. Reporters smoothly moved about like sharks, hungerly awaiting to get the band's reaction to being robbed.

Tolver was being drawn, like everyone else, to their anticipated arrival. The energy of the crowd was pulling him in. Then he spotted Nathan leaning against one of the pillars. He was dressed in his pinstriped jacket and holding a briefcase, looking unassuming and acting as if he too were there waiting for Led Zeppelin's arrival. Nathan was waiting, all right. He was waiting for something far more beneficial. He was waiting for an opportunity.

Tolver approached him as if he were stalking a wild creature. He made his way close enough to reach out, and when he was ready, he tapped Nathan's shoulder, but he took a half step closer to be sure he could speak with him and not make a scene.

Nathan was staring intently out the front doors of the lobby. Tolver could see the gears turning hard in Nathan's head as he studied the police presence outside. He was trying to figure out how to get around them, knowing he was stuck until something gave way.

Tolver reached out and tapped him again, only this time forcefully. Nathan quickly spun around but showed no emotion when he recognized his time-traveling partner.

"Don't do this. You've got to come back."

Nathan just stared at him, his posture unmoving. Upon seeing this, Tolver wanted to ease the tension, "It shouldn't be that much longer before we return."

"There is nothing for me to go back to."

"But you don't belong here."

"How do you know that? How do you know every time this scenario plays out, we aren't the ones who come back in time and steal this money?"

"Because other tourists who have stolen the money as well, so it can't just be us."

"And they spend it before they return. That's the difference between us and them... they go back. Not me.

This is it. I'm willing to take this chance and start a new life."

"But you'll change the course of history."

"That's a bunch of crap. Seriously, I don't think I mean that much in the big picture, at least not enough to make a change the way you are saying. You'll see. When you return, time will have forgotten about me. I won't have made a name for myself at this moment, nor will I have mattered a nickel in the one I came from. And I'm just fine with that."

Tolver was frightened. He didn't want anything to do with Nathan right now. During this trip, Tolver had been alarmed at how Nathan plowed thoughtlessly into social situations, going to the front desk to check in, meandering throughout the hotel, hunting the band's doctor down, and then, the cherry on the cake, bringing the general practitioner back to their room. It may have all happened within the confines of this establishment, but it was as if Nathan were testing those waters for this very moment. He was seeing how far he could push things before they broke, and now, because he hadn't faced any consequences, he confidently carried a wild look of determination in his eyes.

They stared each other down as Tolver desperately tried to figure out his next move.

Then, all at once, the crowd outside began hollering as the band approached in their sleek black limo. Any opportunity Tolver had to peacefully resolve this standoff was disappearing with their rising voices.

Outside, the police and security guards were trying

to keep the fans and press back. Those providing protection maintained a pathway to the front doors for the band and their manager. There were shouts from enthusiastic fans and poignant questions from the press, who had peppered themselves throughout the manic gathering. Photographers took photos with flashbulbs rapidly popping as the group approached the entrance. The crowd was aggressive as people surged forward, with the guards and cops doing their best to push the unruly mob back.

Out of nowhere, a photographer and a news reporter rushed through the lobby on a collision course with the band. Nathan realized it was his best opportunity to make a break for it. He proceeded smoothly by backing into the developing situation. He never took his eyes off Tolver—making sure his cautious friend didn't try to stop him. The news reporter stuck a microphone in Jimmy Page's face and started asking questions about the heist. Page's reaction suggested that this wasn't what he wanted to talk about. He looked exhausted by all this unwanted publicity. The photographer positioned himself to get a shot of the whole group, but just before he snapped the shutter, Nathan backed into him. The photographer stumbled forward, encroaching into the band's space. Peter Grant reacted to this incursion by manhandling the photographer and shoving him to the floor. The reporter was outraged as security guards rushed to keep the journalist from the embattled troupe. Peter finished this confrontation by delivering a few profanities in the reporter's face.

In the meantime, Nathan had rolled off the

photographer and calmly made his way through the excited throng. The crowd parted for him so they could get a better view of the explosive exchange between Zeppelin's manager and the reporter. Tolver's eyes widened as he watched Nathan make his move. He whispered in a desperate plea, "Oh my God, no. Come back!"

Plant, Page, Jones, and Bonham made their way through the lobby, passing right in front of Tolver, who never acknowledged them. The people moved through the lobby like a herd of gazelles trying to keep up with the band. Tolver ignored this weaving bustle of people, staring off into the mob outside, hoping that somehow Nathan would change his mind, that the crowd would part, and he would return.

But that never happened. Nathan disappeared into the night—and the vast expanse of the city.

CHAPTER TWENTY-SIX

THE MAN FROM TAURED

B oone and Minka always found a way to make time for a walk. In the past, they had driven far from their homes to a beach or to hike on a trail, and on occasion, they would even take on the terrain to go camping. Not this time. They were walking through the neighborhood Minka lived in. The stroll didn't make sense to him, especially if they were attempting to keep a low profile with her neighbors, but there they were, ambling along the sidewalks as if nothing was wrong—a marshal and an explorer in the time travel program being seen together out in the open in broad daylight.

This wasn't the only thing that had a quality of being different to Boone. Ever since his rebuild, everything seemed slightly out of place. It was nothing he could put a finger on, but he sensed it. The air had a peculiar density. The sun seemed to be ethereally displaced. The food he ate and the water he drank all had a different flavor. His interactions with people he knew fell into the same shadow category—the suspicious actions of his bosses at the institute after his return, the visit with Johnathan in the healing chamber, and now, the way Minka was acting. All of it was off-kilter.

As they walked, Minka interrupted his thoughts, "Did you even hear what I've been saying?"

"I'm sorry. I didn't?"

"I said, the reason you and I get to pick and choose what we do and where we live is because we donate our organs from the bodies we leave behind. Those organs go to patients in need. It's a contribution that is accredited to our accounts at the institute. So, we've earned the right to choose our assignments."

Boone played it off as if he knew of this, but in reality, it was the first he had ever heard of such a program. To buy time, he tried to agree with everything that was presented to him, "Yes, of course."

"Then why are you acting as if we shouldn't be seen in public?"

"I guess because of old habits, the whole thing doesn't sit well with me."

"In less than a month we will accept our promotions and move in together, and you're expressing reservations now? I don't understand where this resistance is coming from."

"Resistance?"

"Yes. Ever since you've returned, you have been resistant. First, I heard you didn't want to leave the healing chamber and come home, and now you are acting as if you don't want to be seen with me in public."

"I wouldn't say that. You know I want to be with you."

"Then how do you explain the fact that you are at your old place more than you are over here with me? Last week you unpacked most of the boxes we spent weeks packing before you left. We agreed to this move, the both of us selling our houses to get into the new branch of the time travel program. Boone, we were invited."

"Oh yeah, the unpacking… well, it started with me looking for a photo that I had from back at the academy. I was going to show some of the guys at the division. The search just morphed with looking in other boxes."

"So why couldn't you tell me when I asked you that day? You could have easily waited to do that when we moved your stuff to our new home. Instead, you were distant, almost standoffish, looking lost, which is more to the point of you acting different since you've returned."

Boone took a deep breath. It had been a few weeks since he had been released from the healing chamber. During that time, he had been trying to lay low and piece his life back together.

He desperately wanted to talk to her, tell her everything he had been going through, but it was all too unimaginable. How could he talk about the things he was experiencing in his everyday life, their neighborhood, friends, and family; even his job seemed the same, but each one had a different aspect. It was like the memory of the butterfly garden Minka had installed in her backyard. Boone could recall in great detail the koi pond bordered by noninvasive butterfly bushes and patches of Joe-Pye weed. The monarch butterflies migrating north went wild for these plants, so Minka had plenty of them, but now he couldn't find a trace of the plants or the garden. The plot was completed years ago. It was as if she had simply plowed it over—or never had a terrace garden to begin with.

In the middle of these thoughts, he caught her examining him. As soon as he made eye contact, she lashed out. "This is what I'm talking about. We can have a conversation just as long as we don't go too deep. The minute I ask you anything that seems to cross a personal boundary, you clam up."

"I'm sorry. I'm immersed in some things right now."

"Yes, I know. You've told me repeatedly about needing time to sift through these issues while at my home, at your house, or on our walks together. You keep telling me you need space."

"And what's the matter with that?"

"What's the matter? You're cutting me out of your life. You've never acted this way with me before. We've been a team ever since you helped me down that trail and back to your campsite. We've never looked back, never had secrets from each other, until now."

"I know I've been acting funny, but it's just something I need to work through before I can share my thoughts. The time travel program has never been in question, though."

"That's not true. You've had your doubts."

"Questioning things isn't doubting them. I believe in the program."

"Then why won't you put on your bracelet?" Minka held up her wrist to show the sleek black cuff whose series of tiny lights glowed green. "This is what I'm talking about. You've been asked, more than once, to put it on, and you won't. You've fought it every step of the way since your return, and it's not just me who has requested this of you."

"I know I haven't been myself lately, but things will change. I promise. I just need a little more time."

"Wearing this is the only way to stay in the program. Without being plugged into the system, you can't be selected for another mission."

Boone tried to remain calm. He remembered counting down the days until they would release him when he was in the healing chamber. That was the first time his suspicions about something not being quite right were confirmed. When the doctors, technicians, and other medical personnel addressed the information field generator, they didn't call out for Landau... they called out for a thing called Lassiter. The computer would respond to them as Landau, but its tone was different—as if it were preoccupied, controlling a lot of other things. As it got nearer to the end of his stay in the chamber, that's when they sent in the bracelet.

Boone didn't know what to make of the broad, smooth alloy bangle at first. He picked it up from the pass-through drawer as if he were forced to remove a rotting piece of garbage. He looked at the technician through the observation window and asked, "What do you want me to do with this."

"Put it on." The technician smiled broadly as he held up his arm, revealing the one he had fastened to his wrist.

As Boone held it, the band felt a lot lighter than it looked. He told the technician that he'd put it on later. He didn't get an argument, and the man left without saying another word. Placing it on the table caused the bracelet to pop open. Like a clam, it sat there, eagerly waiting for his wrist. The whole setup was wrong. The metal pulled on him, trying to get him to attach it to his being. Boone resisted, and he planned to keep resisting for as long as humanly possible.

Now, he was having to fend Minka off before she made another attempt at delving deeper into his psyche, "Look, I just need more time."

"I want to believe you. I keep waiting for it to happen, but the program doesn't have the same patience as I do. They want results, and they wanted them yesterday. They are falling behind in their conversion goals for this quarter, and part of that failure rests with us."

"What do you mean? Because I haven't put on that bracelet?"

"The only way the bracelets work is through the synthesized organs produced at the institute because of our rebuilds. The computer laces additional coding within our cell structure. The bracelets key on this coding and feed the data back into the system."

"You're telling me I'm gumming up the works

because I'm not wearing that bracelet?"

"When we travel, they harvest our expired body for parts. The more they use our organs in other people, the more of the population they can reach. It's us doing our part and complying with the administration's wishes in creating a more efficient state. When you don't travel, that affects production. When the state doesn't reach its quota, they tend to investigate. After such an audit, they send out recommendations or distribute penalties for those not in compliance. We could lose our status, our new home, and be stuck without a chance to advance."

Boone stood there, taking this all in. The organs they were creating somehow allowed the bracelets to monitor people and possibly control them. It was a lot to try to take in all at once. He whispered as if from a distant memory, "When did the government initiate the program?"

"It came about with the convergence of the information field generators. Very few people were privy to the fact that they had built three of them. Each of these quantum computers had a particular area of expertise. We were associated with the one from the Department of Energy. After the merger, the administration made the push to reshape our nation. The goal now is to get the rest of the world to follow, and it's happening. Our organ donations are a part of that process."

Boone's body shuddered as an icy chill radiated down his backbone. He squinted, looking at the haze of taupe in the air, wondering if it were pollution or the natural color of this atmosphere. If he wanted the chance to leave this ungodly place, he would have to put that bracelet on. The time machine was the only gateway for returning him to what he understood. It was a gamble, though. As soon as he wore that bracelet, those sanctimonious qubits had every possibility of flagging him for being different.

"So, this is Lassiter's ideal world." Boone said it with disgust.

Upon hearing this, Minka snapped at him, "As a species, this ideal world is exactly what we need to survive. The merger turned the population around, made us a more productive culture, saved us from certain societal breakdowns, a behavioral sink, and gave us hope for a more prolific and peaceful planet. For this to work, there must be sacrifices, and we are all expected to make them. It's why we donate our body parts; it's a big reason why we are moving to a new location, for we need to extend the reach of this program."

"I see." His response was less than enthusiastic.

"You don't approve?"

"I didn't say that."

"You didn't have to. It's in your tone." Minka then uttered a beguiled phrase that was foreign to Boone. She hissed and rolled her tongue as if she were a witch casting a spell. Then, she gazed at him as if waiting for a response.

Boone was flummoxed as he desperately tried to figure out what to say.

Minka stared at him, waiting until the growing silence became uncomfortable, "You have no idea what I just said, do you?"

"Language has never been my strong suit. It's why I ask for the upgrade before I go out on a mission." Once stating this, he wished he could have taken it back.

"It is the language of Lassiter. He blessed us with this insight. Those in the know, speak it."

"I can't remember. Maybe it has something to do with my rebuild."

"The rebuild is how the language is introduced."

"There was something about the rebuild, I can't put my finger on it…"

"I know it's been difficult for you since you've returned. They said there was a possibility something had gone wrong in the entanglement corridor, a glitch of some sort, but then you arrived anyway. Since they released you, I've watched and waited for you to come around. They requested that I keep an eye on you. I didn't want to believe, but you aren't going to come around because you can't."

"It's happening. I'm here. I'm ready."

"Since you've returned, you vacillate between being lost and over-eager. It's as if you are trying to shift my attention away from the real issues at hand."

"Real issues? Like what?"

"Playing things off won't work to your advantage

anymore either. They're on to you. I didn't want to believe them, but they were right."

"What do you mean? I've done nothing wrong."

"Then put the bracelet on."

There was a hesitation in Boone that wasn't going away anytime soon.

"I'm sorry, I can't."

"I'm sorry, too."

Her response caught him off guard, and he looked at her puzzled, "What have you done?"

"I had no choice. Looking at you, I swear you are Boone, my Boone, but you aren't. And that means he's out there somewhere, and I can only hope he is doing all he can to get back here."

Suddenly the air around them broke with the rumble of heavy motors racing toward them. Several black sedans screeched to a stop very close to where they both stood. Well-dressed agents began to pour out of the cars, leveling their guns at Boone as they rushed toward him. Minka backed away to give the agents space as they wrestled to control him. One of the agents pulled Boone's sleeve back aggressively, exposing his wrist. Helpless, he watched as Minka stepped forward, reached into her sweater, and pulled out the bracelet he had been refusing to wear. Without looking into his eyes, she placed it on his wrist, locking it. She spoke softly, "I'm sorry, but I need you to be a part of this if I have any chance of getting him back."

It would be the last benevolent gesture he would encounter for quite some time. The indicator lights blinked red as the sharpest of pains took hold of his body. His jaw clenched uncontrollably, grinding his molars roughly together as his nervous system began the process of being rerouted. The surge caused his muscles to tighten and spasm, locking his joints into place. He started to vibrate like thin strands of copper flooded with an overwhelming torrent of electricity. Just before his eyes rolled into the back of his head, he noticed the words inscribed on his bracelet.

Be Here Now.

As they roughed Boone up, they tossed him into the back of a sedan. Minka screamed, "No! Wait! It's not supposed to be like this!"

An agent quickly grabbed her, "You mustn't get in the way. Clearly, he's not well. We need to get him back to the institute for observation."

"You're hurting him. He doesn't know what to do."

"It's out of our hands now."

"But he has done what you asked of him. He wears the bracelet."

"Of what Lassiter asked of him. Of what Lassiter asked from all of us."

Boone tried to speak, but his failed attempt resulted in drool dribbling out of the corner of his mouth. He was helpless, unable to fight. An odd sensation washed over him as Lassiter prepared Boone's body to become a part of the greater good, the Taured. His ability to hear the sounds around him faded. Conversations muffled until they were awash in an ocean of static, and for a brief moment, all those tiny crackling noises eerily sounded like applause at a concert.

CHAPTER TWENTY-SEVEN

YOUR TIME IS GONNA COME

Johnathan Driscoll knew immediately what the alert meant when it came in over his phone. The marshal had been playing in his weekly pinochle game with a few of his closest friends when the call came in, and he politely bowed out. Those alerts weren't to be taken lightly, and he hurried to his vehicle. When a call came in like this, it usually meant someone had decided to cut themselves loose to try to stay in the era they had been sent to—this happened from time to time; an explorer or a tourist thinking they could lose themselves in the period they were visiting. His superiors would have been the ones who pulled the alarm when they got confirmation of such a situation. Every marshal was on edge when summoned because they knew they were the one tasked with hunting the fugitive down.

The virtual particles these people were made of on the other side of the Kolmogrov collectors didn't expire as many scientists had initially predicted. No one could explain why these particles weren't breaking down, but some physicists speculated that the properties in the daughter universes they traveled to were responsible for holding these particles together for longer than anyone could have ever imagined.

His superiors were miffed at how something so irresponsible could happen with all the planning and oversight pouring into each mission and well-rehearsed tourist trip. The senior officials were further aggrieved when they came to the realization that all it took was for one of the marshals to be looking the other way, and then an explorer or tourist could give them the slip. Most of the time, a marshal was able to track the offender down before they could flee too far, but on occasion, one of these temporal trotters—as the marshals liked to refer to the violators—got away.

Disengaging the self-driving mode, Johnathan rocked the wheel of his car from side to side as he slalomed through traffic, wishing he were permitted to use a siren while making his way back to the command center. The aid of flashing red and blue lights accompanied by the wailing sound would have explained his erratic maneuvers to his fellow motorists. Perhaps he was so worked up because, in the back of his mind, he was afraid the name of the person they wanted him to hunt down would be Boone Masterson.

There was a story circulating through the station that Boone hadn't made it back and that the department was trying to cover it up. Johnathan had difficulty believing Boone would leave his post voluntarily—that wasn't who he was—and if Boone had somehow gotten lost, he knew the man would do everything in his power to get back. But if the gossip were true about him not returning, then one day one of these calls would be to a marshal to hunt his friend down.

Johnathan reckoned if Boone's mission were botched, then the tragedy at Tilt Time had to be the cause. The investigators would come to find a citizen had been radicalized by foreign extremists, and parked a truck with explosives right next to the commercial structure. The terror group took advantage of this misguided individual, throwing him the red meat he craved, and redirected his anger. The terrorists were able to strike Tilt Time without ever having to step foot within the country.

The explosion blew half the building apart and triggered another unfortunate event that had been lying dormant at this hub for exceptional sightseers. At the moment Ozman was transmitting the Adinkras of the tourists to Landau, the explosion took place, and the information was rerouted to the backup server on site, which, in turn, transmitted the data.

The semiconductors approved for this backup system were to be vetted through Sand to Silicon, Tolver's place of employment. Unbeknownst to Tolver, when his company accepted an order of high-grade semiconductors to test, those in charge took advantage of the situation and often switched out as many as they could get away with. In this instance, those lower-grade substitute wafers had made their way to the backup system at Tilt Time. Those committing these acts of theft waited to do the switch until after Tolver gave his stamp of approval. They had Tolver on record as validating the authenticity of the batch. He was the designated fall guy for anything that went wrong. The inferior chips relayed data sets that degraded some of the Adinkras of the tourists and essentially locked Boone out of his assignment, giving the information field generator free rein to deposit the marshal wherever Landau wished.

Still, there were rumors of Boone being seen on campus.

The phone rang in Johnathan's car, and he pressed a button on his steering wheel in response. Before he could glance at the readout, Vance McMillan was on the other end of the call, sounding rather perturbed. Johnathan had very few interactions with the chief operations officer, but each of those contacts always left him feeling as if there was more than he was being asked to do. He took a deep breath before he answered, "Hello, Mr. McMillan."

"Mr. Driscoll, I see you were tapped for tracking down our fugitive."

"Yes, sir. I'm heading into the station now."

"As you should be. I don't have to remind you that these are delicate situations, each has its own special nuance, but this particular case has to be handled differently."

"Should I swing by your office before heading to the STAR facility?"

"No, that won't be necessary. The only thing you need to know about this tourist is that I cannot have his memories sent back to infect our timeline."

There was a slight pause as Johnathan tried to deduce what Vance was asking of him, "I think I see what you are getting at, and it shouldn't be a problem, sir."

"Do you see what I'm getting at, Mr. Driscoll? Because once you bag your suspect and destroy those Kolmogrov collectors, you won't be returning, either. It's a leap of faith. Do you understand?"

There was a longer stretch of silence as the request

hit home, "Yes, sir. I understand."

"Good. Remember, there is nothing we can do for you here until you've fulfilled everything about your mission on the other side." Vance hung up before Johnathan could utter another word.

Driving toward the neoteric station within the high-tech campus of Brookhaven, Johnathan felt a little queasy, for it was beginning to dawn on him exactly what McMillan was asking. He wasn't just assassinating this fugitive; he was assassinating himself. There was a cycle for how things worked within the program—this loop was essential from start to finish. His arrival back at Brookhaven was the proof of his existence—and he was going to interrupt it.

He would be casting himself into the sands of time and having to trust that one day in the future, they would summon up his Adinkra and rebuild him just as he was right now.

CHAPTER TWENTY-EIGHT

OVER THE HILLS AND FAR AWAY

Tolver struggled to climb up the few dozen stairs of the public library. He was determined to visit this place of literary enlightenment as many times during the week as possible. He had become obsessed with this regime ever since his release from the mental rehab facility. Although the doctors had insisted his travel through time had gone well, he had been dealing with several nagging physical complications. It was a constant battle between his flare-ups of arthritis, shortness of breath, and the slow and steady deterioration of his vision. This last ailment troubled him most as he insisted on re-examining the newspapers on file. Tolver found himself needing stronger and stronger reading glasses, and no matter the optometrist he spoke to, there was nothing they could do to correct his vision.

The reason most of his medical issues hadn't been fixed for so long was because no one knew who was to blame. The insurance companies were still sorting through the whole affair, their efforts were to determine if it was Tilt Time or the stint he served in the asylum.

His account of Nathan leaving the Drake Hotel and disappearing into the night didn't sit well with anyone upon his return. It was too difficult for them to believe—especially the branch of law enforcement tasked with overseeing Tilt Time. Regardless of the opportunities he was given to recant his story, he never budged from the facts. Tolver repeatedly stated he watched as Nathan walked right out the front doors of the Drake, with the loot, into the bustling streets of New York City. Tolver had his account of what happened, and that clashed with the government's impeccable record of never losing a man to the time travel program. The pristine record was hammered home by scientist after scientist as they were called to the witness stand. They all stated the physical reality of no one being able to stay in the era they had traveled to.

The more Tolver was insistent on what had transpired on his journey, the crazier they made him look. The government argued Tolver was fabricating his story and countered it with one of their own. After Tolver had been disgraced and fired from his job at Sand to Silicon, the lawyers kept piling on. He was painted to be untrustworthy and unstable, a menace to society, and in the end, this was all the justification the judge needed in committing Tolver.

The official report stated that Nathan was lost in the Tilt Time explosion. It was a line of crap that didn't sit right with Tolver. Although he tried, he couldn't rely on any of the others in the group to back up his story. No one else would swear they saw Nathan leave the lobby of the Drake.

As time passed, the group grew apart. Mallory disappeared into the folds of the company, never to be heard from again. Slater was in and out of so many surgeries he never seemed to be able to concentrate on anything but whatever rehab he was going through. Rowen had grown to hate the very concept of time travel, becoming a harsh critic and vehemently protesting out on the streets every chance he got.

Throughout Tolver's entire stint at the psychiatric ward, they tried to move the needle on his story by locking him in a straitjacket, drugging him, and even using electroshock therapy. He incurred pain. In the process he lost teeth, they damaged his eyesight, and eventually some of his motor skills. Through all of it, he never deviated from the facts as he knew them. The reality was Nathan had left them. This was the reason Tolver kept hobbling back to the library. He was looking to prove his version of the story. Arriving armed with his reading glasses, eye drops, a notepad, and a brown bag lunch, he spent countless hours combing through the chronicles looking for any trace of Nathan's existence.

He knew most that worked at the library thought him mad, but because of this no one ever really bothered him.

Down in the library's lower levels, in the confines of the room that contained the archive viewing machines, Tolver found something—a few articles on a fiscal incident that happened in Livingston County, Michigan, in 1974. It was the closest thing he ever got to an answer.

CHAPTER TWENTY-NINE

TANGERINE

A s the sun made its way up and over the horizon, its light pierced the trees and left long orange streaks that stripped the ashen cement of the roadway. The squad car sped along Highway 95 as a call came squawking in over the radio. Trooper Hal Gritchen, who was nearing the end of his shift, and was passing Oceola Township on his way back to Lansing, reluctantly responded. The dispatcher directed him to the home of Duane Willsmore, who reported an unusual find while he was out squirrel hunting.

The black and white Dodge Monaco cruiser sped over the paved roads in response to the call. Trooper Gritchen pulled into the gravel driveway behind a two-tone copper and white Chevrolet pickup truck. Willsmore was already waiting for him with the screen door open. The man couldn't have been more than twenty-two. He was still dressed in his hunting garb, wearing a flat-billed cap, red flannel jacket, brown shirt, caramel-colored coveralls, and scuffed-up work boots. It had been a while since he had seen a haircut or bothered to trim his beard. His physical appearance embraced the youth and carefree spirit of the sixties. Willsmore could afford to cultivate this look. The fact he was a homeowner told the trooper this young man took his responsibilities seriously. When questioned why he had time to hunt on the weekday, it was revealed Willsmore was one of the independent truckers striking across the nation because of the oil embargo the OPEC nations had levied against the country.

After a brief exchange about the embargo, they made their way through the house to the kitchen. On the back porch, a pair of squirrels were hanging from a hook mounted next to the rear entrance. Their placement on the hook was so obvious; it was as if they were hung there to prove Willsmore had been hunting earlier that morning. The trooper spotted the aluminum suitcase sitting on the table. A relatively recent design, it was pretty dinged up and scratched as if it had seen a lot of action in its short life. A crowbar sat on the table next to it.

The trooper pointed at the tool, "Was that found with it?"

"No. I was contemplating opening it. The case has combination locks by the latches. The more I considered opening it, the more I hesitated for fear of what I might find. I thought it better to have a witness to whatever was inside. That's when I phoned for you."

"And you said you found this while you were hunting?"

"Yes. I had bagged a couple squirrels and was working my way across the edge of the Powell property. I got near a tree that looked like it had been struck by lightning a few years back. There was a pile of small branches, and as I stepped on them to cross the area, I heard what sounded like wood hitting metal. It didn't take much work to dig this up. To tell you the truth, it looked to be placed in haste."

"Why would you say that?"

"Well, the hole it was in was more of a depression. It wasn't buried that deep. There were more branches and leaves covering the case than any meaningful amount of dirt."

"Did you cause all this damage getting it out?"

"I may have put a dent in here or there when I stepped on it, but other than that, this is exactly how I found it."

Gritchen nodded and tilted the suitcase up so he could see the combination locks. He tried the latches, then rested the case on its edge and used the crowbar to unfasten the locks. Once he had loosened the clasps, he set the crowbar down and placed the case back on its side.

Working it open revealed stacks of bills held together with thick rubber bands, folded maps of both Pennsylvania and Ohio and a pair of blue velvet gloves. The case was full of these bundles of cash, with no rhyme or reason for how they were stacked.

The trooper looked at Willsmore, who had gasped at the find, "You made the right decision by calling this in."

What followed was eight years of legal battles with the owner of the Powell property where the case had been found, Willsmore, and Livingston County—all wanting their cut. The story would eventually make the national papers, but in all that time, no one could ever say where the money had come from.

Willsmore always insisted there was something about the way he found the holdall that left the impression it was buried in haste. Even after all those years, as the case was being litigated and with the additional attention from the national press, no one ever came forward to claim the aluminum suitcase full of cash.

It was as if everything the mysterious individual was ever about had simply vanished.

Novels by

R. Vincent Tibbetts

Red Planet Pioneer

The year is 2079, and colonizing Mars is about to become a very dangerous business. Corporations are the drivers of a process that governments desperately want to regulate. Investors expect massive profits from taking such risks. With the world teetering on global catastrophe, Xavier Pentagrass has been sent to Mars to run the Red Planet Pioneer Corporation. As all are about to find out, it will soon become his personal cause.

The technology driving the colonization process is the development of a new android race known as Dextoids. Breakthroughs in quantum computing have allowed for their manifestation. Humanity has grown to rely upon these creations for every single facet of its existence.

Out in the barren plains of Mars, two Dextoids have escaped their minders. Their extensive knowledge can't prepare them for freedom. Unhinged from humanity, they will shape the attitude for how the Red Planet will be colonized and how mankind will treat the Dextoid population for years to come.

A genetically engineered adventure, welcome to Red Planet Pioneer.

The Descent from Anvil

On a world where the days are ticking toward extinction, the desperate inhabitants send their best emissaries into the unknown for a solution.

Coiled in the distrust of the Cold War and faced with an enigma that threatens humanity, three ordinary people wage an extraordinary fight to bridge the fissure between worlds to save a people they cannot comprehend. Every action they take ripples through time in a macabre dance of destiny and determination.

The Concierge

Marteen has dreams, aspirations and absolutely no idea what he's doing or what he's up against. Marteen lives in a world where those who can find a connection with the wealthy and powerful are rewarded, the rest linger in abject poverty. Marteen has a loose plan to escape his limited life in this top-heavy society. There is one job within the confines of the metropolis that can raise him above his static station. Determined to achieve his goal, Marteen embarks on a chaotic and bumbling journey through the concrete class system epitomizing the phrase, be careful what you wish for. Welcome to the arcane and Kafkaesque world of The Concierge.

An Instance of Opposition

In a world where the government maintains power by teetering on ecological disasters and the onslaught of war, Tindra Hightower and Clive Vanderjack collide. The seemingly random actions of a reckless hierarchy bring them together, and the events which unfold force them to flee from the long arm of the State. With Tindra's knowledge of hacking and Clive's skills as a government operative, they find themselves immersed in a bureaucratic imbroglio with deadly consequences. Forging a fragile alliance on their roller coaster ride, they brave their battles with their blended sights set on the only real prize— their freedom.

R. Vincent Tibbetts was raised in Western Pennsylvania during the 1970's. It was a time when their professional football team captured the heart of a city. It was because of this that the surrounding areas immersed itself in a culture of winning. However, those feelings changed with the death of the steel industry. Witnessing the economic shockwave ripple through these communities from the gutting of such an industrial expanse had an impact on his psyche. It led him to see his surroundings in a new light. He grew to have an appreciation for how things worked, the workings of the natural world, and developing a mindset for conservation.

His interests in art, photography, and film production brought him to California and a career in the entertainment business, where he is a Chief Lighting Technician and Studio Electrician.

He is an entrepreneur at heart.

His hobbies include beach volleyball, softball, golf, hiking, camping, and surfing.

He resides in Seal Beach, California.

www.ingramcontent.com/pod-product-compliance
Lightning Source LLC
Chambersburg PA
CBHW061957170626
46813CB00006B/2671